OCTOBEARFEST

RENAISSANCE SHIFTERS
BOOK ONE

MURPHY LAWLESS

a miz kit production

OCTOBEARFEST

ISBN-13 (e-book): 978-1-83557-030-2

ISBN-13 (print): 978-1-83557-031-9

Cover Artist: Malice & Mayhem Book Covers

CHAPTER 1

*B*eing an adult sucked.

Bill Torben didn't like to think of himself as a complainer. In fact, he thought of himself as a good-natured, get-on-with-things kinda guy. But things had been lurching along from okay to bad to worse for the past few years, and as far as he could tell, he was the only one in his family who was concerned about any of that.

It was fair enough that his parents had stepped out of the ring, as far as running Thunder Bear Brewery and the accompanying brew pub was concerned. They'd started it in their early twenties, and were retirement age now. God knew they'd earned that retirement, between raising four boys and developing an award-winning IPA along the way. But Steve, the next oldest and next-most-reliable brother, had moved away years ago now, and the younger two...

The two youngest Torbens, Jon and Laurie, were great. Charming, good-looking, funny—God knew the women thought so—and terrific performers. But *serious* and *responsible* weren't words that Bill would apply to them, and it didn't seem to matter how often he explained that renaissance faires were *fun*, but also expensive and drew time and attention from running the brewery itself.

Bill couldn't exactly blame them. He'd been as into it as they were, up until just a few years ago. Before he'd started taking over more of the family business. And he missed it, especially when the younger brothers came home sweaty and slightly sunburned and happy from days of selling brew at the faires, but...it didn't deal with the day to day realities of running a small business.

Sometimes he wished he'd done what Steve had done: move to another state, start his own business, find love, and get married.

A low chuckle shook his shoulders. The truth was, probably half his grumbling right now was that Steve had gotten married the past summer. He and his mate were a wonderful pair, and Bill was happy for them. What had gotten under his skin was that their cousin, who'd come up from Australia for the wedding, had *also* found his fated mate about ten seconds after arriving in small-town Virtue, New York, which was half the size of Renaissance, Colorado and apparently just *teeming* with love waiting to happen. Bill wanted to find that for himself.

Unfortunately for him, he was currently awaiting a 73-year-old jazz musician who had been married longer than Bill himself had been alive. She was the main event for the upcoming Octoberfest that the brewery held annually, and even if she wasn't going to be his true love, Bill was looking forward to meeting her. He'd been listening to her music for years.

A knock sounded on the office door, startling him out of his grim examination of the books. He glanced at his phone: ten to two. Gwendolyn Brooker was early, but that was a hell of a lot better than late, by Bill's standards. He started tidying the desk, calling, "Come in!" and stood with a practiced smile and an offered hand as the door opened.

No, as the door *flew* open, bouncing all the way to the wall and off it again with a protesting squeak of its hinges.

The woman who blew in was as unlike the sedate, white-haired pictures of Gwendolyn Brooker as Bill could imagine.

She was tall. Rangy. Massive amounts of wild, rough-cut dark hair that was currently tied up in what could only be considered a punk-rock ponytail. Winged eyeliner like knives, haunting vividly blue eyes. Cheekbones that could cut, and a mouth slashed with a drinkable wine red lipstick. She wore rows of hoop earrings and a choker necklace of black lace with a plunging pendant that fell into the cleavage of a hand-cut *Ramones* t-shirt beneath a studded leather jacket. Multiple belts fell in silver-punctured loops around her hips, and her blue jeans were torn at the knees, one of which sported a bandage with blood staining through the absorbent layer, making it clear the torn-out knees had been come by honestly. She wore thick black boots with untied laces, and carried an electric guitar slung over her shoulder like a weapon.

She was *fabulous*. She was *magnificent*. She was *electrifying*.

She was, unquestionably, his fated mate.

And, Bill knew with a sinking feeling, she was going to ruin *everything*.

CHAPTER 2

It wasn't that Gwen hadn't played bars before. God, no, she'd played more of them than she could count. But most of the time those bars had a certain vibe to them, and that vibe was "ew."

The Thunder Bear Brewpub was about as far from "ew" as could possibly exist in a bar. It was only mid-afternoon, so there weren't crowds hanging around, which let the broad, log-cabin-style exterior walls gleam gold in the autumn sunlight. The main doors were flung open, giving the place a welcoming air, and there was a delightful-looking maze of outdoors beer gardens with corrugated plastic roofing that looked like it was either new or kept religiously clean. The beer gardens all had half walls with plexiglass windows ranging from all the way closed to all the way open. The seating, made up of benches and bar stools with tables to match their heights, had suspiciously comfortable-looking cushions. They came off the seats: Gwen could see the ties that held them in place. She bet they got industrial-washed at least once a week, and for some reason that pleased her, so she was smiling as she went into the main building.

Like the exterior, it was open, clean, smelled good, and had a friendly feel to it. There were a few people around, staff working behind the bar, tidying up, raising their eyebrows to see if she needed seating or a drink or anything, and going back to work but keeping an eye on her when she indicated she was okay. A handful of patrons were scattered comfortably around the interior seating, like they were in a place where everybody knew their name. One lifted his chin in greeting, and a woman gave her a curious look, which was fair. Gwen didn't, at a glance, look like she fit in with the local crowd.

Which was fair enough, as she was neither local nor even all that fond of beer, so a place known for its home brews generally wasn't her scene.

The entirely decent stage set up at one end of the biggest room *was* her scene, though. Wonderfully, it didn't have any chicken wire, either rolled up or already hanging down, to protect the musicians from bottles being thrown by the audience. That, Gwen thought, was a great sign. She'd played at way too many dives where getting beer bottles thrown at her was just part of the job. She nosed around a bit, checked the time, went to use the bathroom—also clean, smelling like lemon, and with mirrors that were neither warped, cracked, nor weirdly yellow from cheap backing. "I love this place," she informed her reflection as she washed her hands, then bopped back on out to the main room, skidding the soles of her boots across the floor to see how the traction was.

Good, just like everything else in this place. Not that Gwen was planning to have to make a run for it, but it had happened before, and she liked to be prepared. She went over to one of the staff. "Hey, I've got an appointment with Bill Torben…?"

The woman, white, in her forties, and with the practiced disinterest of long-time bar staff, looked her up and down. "Really?"

"Yeah, at two. Gwen Booker."

"Wow." The woman looked Gwen up and down again, taking a particularly long moment to examine the electric guitar she had slung over her shoulder. "Not what I was expecting when he booked you, but okay, sure. If you head back past the bathrooms, the hallway takes a left and there's a staff door there. Go through it and Bill's office is the last door."

Gwen was used to not being what people expected, so she just grinned, said, "Thanks," and scooted herself on through the staff door and down the hall toward Bill Torben's office. She knocked briskly, heard a "*Come in!*" and pushed the door open with the thrill of excitement that always came before a performance, even if it was just a one-man 'meet the guy who hired you' show.

To her horror, the door flew open like it had been waiting its whole life just for this moment. Like it had been practicing a vigorous swing that would slam it all the way into the wall and bounce it back again like a freight truck. Gwen slapped her hand up, catching the door before it smashed into her face, but honestly, the fact that she'd been able to do that was a freaking *miracle*, because the guy standing up at the far side of the room was the most *ridiculously* attractive human being Gwen had ever laid eyes on.

He was 'toll and *thicc*,' in the parlance of her tweenage niece. Like, *toll*-toll, one of the tallest guys Gwen had ever personally met, maybe six five or so, and he was built like a brick outhouse. There was no particular taper from his shoulder to his hip: he was just *lorg*, as Cindy would also say. Barrel-chested, thick-thighed, *huge* hands. Gwen found herself focusing on the hand he'd reached out toward her as soon as she'd opened the door. It would engulf her own hand. She could think of some really incredible things to do with those thick fingers. The dude could use her for biceps curls, was all she was saying. She lurched forward and put her hand in his.

Yep. Engulfed. Also suddenly very warm and comfortable, like her hand belonged in his and always had. Gwen started to smile without really meaning to, gazing up at this huge, magnificent mountain of a man. He had tremendously thick dark blonde hair in a remarkable pompadour, and a beard that was just thiii-iiis much more than scruff. His deep-set dark blue eyes, strong nose, and wide mouth suited his face perfectly.

He also, she realized, had an expression of increasing dismay stretching the lines of his face longer and longer as he looked her up and down. "G...Gwendolyn Brooker?" The way he said it told Gwen he knew that wasn't right, but that he was desperately hoping he was somehow wrong.

Gwen kind of rolled her eyes, glancing around the room to see if anybody else was there, and offered him a crooked smile in return. "Uh, no? Gwen. Gwen *Booker*."

All the hope drained out of the big man's face. He let go of her hand, put his face in both of his, and moaned, "Oh *no*," into his palms.

Gwen froze, feeling suddenly a bit like a mouse that had alarmed an elephant. "Wh…aaaaat did I do?"

"Oh, no," he said, still into his palms, "no, it was me. Or someone on my staff, but…me. I'm the buck. It stops here. Oh, God, we're doomed."

"That," Gwen said, cautiously, "seems insulting."

Bill Torben—she *assumed* this giant of a man was Bill Torben, anyway—jerked his gaze up from his palms with an expression of overwhelming guilt. "Oh, God, no, not you, I mean, yes, you, you're a *disaster*, but no, not *you*."

Gwen did the look-around-the-room thing again, moving just her eyes until she was pretty certain there wasn't anyone else in there. It was a six by ten room, give or take, dominated—well, *dominated* by the very large man in it, but in furniture terms, dominated by a desk and a wall of filing cabinets that seemed very retro but she felt in her soul were probably incredibly organized. There was a painting she'd only glimpsed on the opposite wall. She had the impression it was of a grizzly bear. A window with closed curtains was behind the desk, which was a shame, because it made the room seem smaller and darker than it needed to be, but on the other hand, if the curtains were open, the sun would glare on his computer monitor.

There was not, unless they were hidden under the desk, anyone else in the room. Once Gwen was satisfied of that, she looked back up at the distraught pub owner. "Still pretty sure I'm insulted."

"I hired *Gwendolyn Brooker*," Bill groaned. "A *jazz musician*. Or at least, I meant to. I don't know what went wrong, oh, *God*." He left Gwen standing in the middle of the room and went back to his desk, shuffling through neatly-arranged paperwork. Gwen stared at him a moment, then several moments, and when it became clear he was going to be busy for some time, shrugged her guitar off her shoulder, leaned it against the filing cabinets, and sat in one of the two chairs on *this* side of the desk, meant for visitors.

After a couple of seconds she made a face, got up, and tried the other chair. It wasn't any more comfortable than the first one had been. "You don't get a lot of people in here, do you?"

"What? No. What?" Bill looked up from the paperwork, his eyebrows—thick, like the rest of him, and darker blonde than his hair—beetled down. "What?"

"These are incredibly uncomfortable chairs," Gwen said with a degree of patient amusement. "Both of them. Like, exceptionally uncomfortable. Nobody sits in them, do they?"

"No, not—not really, no. We actually do most of our business out front, this is just, I thought Ms. Brooker would be more comforta...are they really that bad?"

Gwen's eyebrows lifted. "Have you never sat in one?"

Bill made a vague gesture at himself. At his backside, specifically. Gwen tilted sideways a few inches as if that would remove the desk and allow her to see said backside. "My big ass doesn't fit in most chairs, so I assumed they were more comfortable for other people."

Gwen had only had a brief look at the ass in question, as he'd gone back around the desk. To her mind, it had filled out his jeans *extremely* nicely. "Flying must be no fun for you, then."

"Oh, I don't fly. Bears walk. Uh." A look of horror came over his face and he shook himself. "Uh, I mean, drive? We...I have a commercial license, I drive the delivery trucks sometimes. Who *are* you?" The last words came out plaintively, like he was painfully aware of having messed everything, including this conversation, up. "I mean, Gwen Booker, I got that, but..."

"I'm a rock musician," Gwen said, taking pity on him. "I don't know Gwendolyn Brooker at all, and I don't know a note of jazz music. I'm sorry, dude."

"Bill," he said absently, and then horror crossed his face again. "I didn't even introduce myself, did I? Bill. Bill Torben."

"I figured," Gwen said dryly. "Nice to meet you, Bill. You're very tall. I'm sorry. That was a stupid thing to say."

To her relief, he laughed. A warm, deep laugh that wasn't very loud, but rumbled right across her skin and raised excited goosebumps. "I am tall," he agreed. "Biggest of my brothers, although Steve gives me a run for my money. You're very small."

Gwen laughed. "I'm not. Not really. But from your height probably everybody shorter than a linebacker looks small."

He scratched the side of his jaw, then kept scratching, like his beard itched now that he'd noticed it. "I was a linebacker in high school," he admitted. "You?"

"Funnily enough, I didn't play any football in high school. There was a girl at my school who did, through," Gwen remembered suddenly. "She was hot. Played quarterback. Fast. Great hands. Apparently. I never found out, myself."

To her astonishment, a blush shot up Bill Torben's face, starting from somewhere beneath his t-shirt collar, curdling his neck and then his cheekbones and forehead a deep red that she would have bought as a lipstick shade. Gwen's lips parted in astonishment, and, as his blush held on, turned to a grin. "So now you've met Gwen Booker, rock star and prone to saying inappropriate things at job interviews. Although I guess this isn't really an interview, since I've already been hired."

"We don't *do* rock at Oktoberfest," Bill said desperately. "I don't know how this happened, and I'm sorry, it's not your fault, but we're going to lose our whole audience because of you."

CHAPTER 3

Those were not the words Bill wanted to hear himself say to Gwen Booker. He *wanted* to hear himself say *you're magnificent, you're beautiful, you're exciting, I want to pick you up and hug you—*

A bear hug? his bear asked excitedly. It was a pretty laid-back soul animal, from what Bill could tell about other shifters' animals, but it *loved* hugs. Really truly *loved* them. And it had never quite gotten its fuzzy head around the idea that a bear hug from an actual bear was very alarming to humans, since they used the phrase so affectionately. 'He gave me a bear hug when we saw each other again! I missed him so much!' That kind of thing. His bear was absolutely convinced humans wanted nothing more than to hug *it*, in its huge, furry, claw-y, dangerous natural form.

A bear hug, he agreed somewhat reluctantly. *But a human one, buddy, okay?*

The bear, somewhere between sullen and sad, mumbled, *It's not a bear hug then. It's a human hug,* and mooped back into silence. Bill genuinely felt sorry for it.

"Look, it's not your fault," he said, half to the bear and also entirely to Gwen. "I'm the one who screwed up by booking you. It's just our clientele..." He sank into his seat and rubbed his hands over his face.

"You run a brewhouse," Gwen said hopefully. "You must have a lot of people who like rock?"

Sinking in his chair wasn't enough. Bill actually felt a need to lean forward and put his head against the desk, thumping it a few times for good measure. "You'd think," he said hollowly, to his feet, which he could see now, what with his forehead being on the desk. "And I don't know, maybe we do. But my folks—they started the brewhouse—they made October Jazz a *thing* in this town. There's a whole festival next week. We kind of launch it with the Oktoberfest weekend here at the pub, and then...yeah..."

He dared to glance up, and found Gwen's whole expression basically turned upside-down in consternation. "Oh. Oh, yeah, that's bad then. You have...oh, God. You probably have tickets sold for Gwendolyn Brooker, too, don't you?"

"So many tickets. She's astonishing, really, unbelievable on the horns, plays piano, sings, just basically a one-woman wonder. I've listened to all of her albums and honestly, getting her was actually kind of a coup— oh. Oh, no wonder she was available. It was because I booked you. I mean. I'm sorry, but...it was because I booked you."

Gwen winced. "I'm a working musician, but...yeah,

I'm afraid I'm not so solidly booked up that it'd be any kind of miracle to get me. Sorry about that."

"No, no." Bill sat back up again, pulling his hands down his face. "Not your fault. I got so excited that you —she—was available I didn't check carefully enough, obviously. I should have known I'd need to go through a manager. I think I just found your website, though." He reached for his phone, typing in *gwendolyn brooker*, and the first thing that came up was a dot-com for Gwen Booker. Two results later was a social media presence for Gwendolyn Brooker. With a mortified groan, he turned the phone toward Gwen to show her. "Yep. I took the first hit and didn't realize it wasn't the same person."

Gwen reached across the desk and took his phone like she had every business doing so, flicking through the search results. "In your defense, a decent manager would have her website structured so that mistake couldn't possibly happen, but it looks like her actual domain name lapsed ages ago. I know it makes me a weird old fogey, but I think businesses should have active websites that *aren't* on social media."

"You are neither old nor weird," Bill said, surprising himself with his passion, and surprising Gwen even more. She laughed and shook her head.

"Not that old. Kind of weird, though. Definite fogey, in terms of online presence. My mom was, is, a web designer," she added with an explanatory wave of her hand. "She has whole hours-long rants about how you shouldn't let a handful of billionaire-owned social media companies define your entire online presence. I guess some of it's rubbed off. I have a *band*, Bill. If it was just me, I'd be willing to try to figure something out to help you here, but there are four more people counting on this gig. Also, didn't you notice you were booking a *band* and not just an individual?"

"Gwendolyn Brooker has a band, too," Bill said helplessly. "I was surprised it was only the five of you, in fact. I thought it would be seven."

"Oh, well." Gwen threw her hands upward. Her fingernails were painted black, and the polish was chipped. It was, Bill thought, the sexiest nail polish he'd ever seen. Everything about Gwen Booker was throbbingly hot, including the baffled empathy currently writ large across her face. "You really blew it," she said sympathetically. "How are we gonna make this work? My band will be here tomorrow."

"I don't know. I'm going to have to tell my parents, and call everybody who's got a ticket—"

"You *must* be able to email them, or text," Gwen interrupted incredulously. "Are your sales through one of the online vendors?"

"Most of them." Bill blinked at her as she made another explosive gesture. Apparently she did nothing by halves, including waving her hands around.

"All right, look. So yes, the first thing you have to do is let people know. I'd start by offering a discount for having booked the wrong person but if they want to come anyway, like, here's five bucks off, or a free beer. Free beer would be easier, actually. I bet a shit ton of people will show up anyway just for the beer. Send everybody a voucher with a QR code for a free beer, and let them know their tickets will be refunded or they can cancel if that's what they'd rather. And I know I've already got some Fits coming to the show—"

"Some what?"

Gwen flashed a smile of those wine-red lips, and Bill thought she could wreck him with that mouth. By smiling! By *smiling*, he told himself, and tried extremely hard not to think about what he might otherwise have meant.

Extremely hard was the operative term at the moment, though. Thank God he was sitting behind the desk.

"The Fits. Our fans. The band is the Sixty Pix, the fans say they pitch sixty fits when they see us, they ended up calling themselves 'The Fits,'" Gwen said ruefully. "It's silly, but it's unique, at least. Anyway, so if we can get an idea of how many people might show up anyway I can offer some kind of 'hey meet the artist' thing to pull some of my fans from farther away than they might otherwise come, even on short notice. Last minute and weekend getaway tickets should be available about now anyway. Now, what's the music scene like in Renaissance, anyway? Jazzy, apparently, but there's got to be more than just jazz here, right?"

"I…have no idea?"

Gwen Booker gave him a hard stare. And there was that word again, hard. Bill really needed to avoid it. He swallowed and tried not to squirm under Gwen's grim expression. "You don't know anything about the music scene in the town you live in?"

"I don't think there is much of one?" Bill hesitated.

"No, there must be. My brothers go out a lot. I just... don't."

"Don't go out?"

He gestured at the office, but meant the whole brewpub with the motion. A much smaller motion than Gwen would have made, he thought, but if he waved his hands around like she did, he'd knock lights out of their sockets and break windows. "Not really, no. I keep this place running, and that's about all I have time for."

She really had a magnificent stare. It rivaled his mother's for the *what the hell, Bill?* it implied. Unlike his mother, though, after a moment's consideration, Gwen's cut-glass blue gaze softened and she said, "Then we're going to have to get you out of here and check it out."

"Check what out?"

"Renaissance, Colorado!" Gwen made another of those expansive gestures and grinned at him. "The music scene specifically, but look, we've got a day and a half to turn this around, and we can't do that from inside an office where we don't know anything about the territory! Let's make this happen, big man!"

A twitch went through Bill's...soul...at the phrase *big man,* and he was pretty sure a blush hit him for the second time in fifteen minutes. Gwen's grin got wider. Much, much wider. Bill blushed harder, until he was sure he would no longer embarrass himself if he stood up. That was something, at least. "You're...are you real?"

She's real, his bear said happily. *She's our mate. She's exactly what you need.*

Bill was almost certain that was true. He loved his family, all of them, but not even his parents were as take-charge as Gwen Booker seemed to be, and it felt like Bill had been transported to the Twilight Zone. He'd just been desperately wishing that *somebody* in his life would want to get things done as much as he did.

He just hadn't expected that person to be a wrong hire who came bursting through the door, destined to be the love of his life.

Gwen made a show of pinching herself in a couple places, then raised her dark eyebrows at him. "Pretty sure I'm real. C'mon, let's get that update out to everybody who's bought tickets. Do you know how to make a QR code? Obviously not," she said to his expression. "All right, let me at it." She sprang out of her chair, rubbed her bottom, and made a face at the chair as she came around to Bill's side of the desk. "Up. Or let me sit in your lap, your call."

Bill scrambled out of his chair so fast it was embarrassing, but he would absolutely not be responsible for his body's responses if she sat in his lap, and this was enough of a disaster already. He had no idea how he would explain to this literal rock star of a woman that he, boring old Bill Torben, brewhouse master and general stick-in-the-mud, was meant to be with her for the rest of their lives. Or that he could turn into an incredibly enormous grizzly bear, for that matter, but honestly, that seemed less unlikely than her wanting to stay with him forever.

Gwen plonked down in his chair. "Oh, that's *much* more comfortable. My ass isn't going to be perforated by springs, in this chair. Okay, what's your computer passwo—" The question dissolved into an 'uh' and a burst of laughter and Gwen pushed back from the desk, waving at the computer. "Sorry, I'm not actually that rude. Or I am, but I caught myself in time. Mostly. Please put your password in?"

Bill lurched forward and typed his password in with the largest, clumsiest hands that had ever existed. It took him four tries. It wasn't even a hard password. He stepped back again, actually shaking with effort, and with the warm, slightly spicy scent of Gwen Booker in his nose. She smelled *so* good. He wanted to put his nose in her neck and just breathe for about a week.

Instead he pretended he was a perfectly normal human being who didn't do weird things like that, and said, "There?" hopefully.

"Great, okay, let me just generate a coupon code to link the QR code to, and then…no, just a one-off, you piece of electronic horseshooooe." Her gaze flickered to him as she avoided swearing, as if he might be horribly shocked by her using an actual curse word. He sucked his cheeks in, trying not to laugh, and her gaze darkened with obviously-mocking threat before she turned her attention back to the computer. "Okay, look, I'm going to associate it with the brewpub's website, okay? You've got one, right?" Gwen's hands flew over the keyboard, filling things out, creating stuff Bill had no idea how to do, typing notes and drafts and finally sitting back with an, "Et voila! All right, we've just got to send it to the ticket vendor to propagate. You want to take a look at what I've done first?"

"I can see you've spelled everything right," Bill said faintly. "I'm not sure there's anything else I'm capable of doing besides gawking in appreciation."

She laughed and submitted the draft she'd written. "Okay then. That's stage one of 'Save Oktoberfest' underway. Stage two is seeing what this town's got to offer and where we can advertise locally!" She stood up with the same energy she'd demonstrated doing everything else, and Bill had a sudden, vivid interest in how she would express that energy in bed.

Which was so far from an okay thing to be thinking he actually kicked himself in his own shin. His bear, startled, said, *Ow!* even though it hadn't really hurt, and Bill mumbled a silent, half-hearted apology to the offended animal. Gwen, having seen the whole kicking himself thing, blinked at him in confusion, and Bill shook his head. "Nothing. It's just that you're the most amazing women I've ever met."

Gwen Booker looked him up and down with a smile that bordered on a leer, then winked. "Oh, honey, you ain't seen nothing yet."

CHAPTER 4

Gwen was *almost* certain—by which she meant absolutely totally certain—that Bill hadn't kicked himself because she was amazing, although he wasn't wrong: she was pretty damn cool. She was also certain he wasn't going to tell her whatever it was he'd really been thinking, although from the way he'd blushed and blushed and *blushed* at her 'big man' comment, she bet she had some pretty solid ideas on where his mind had been in general.

She hoped so, anyway, because her own mind was trawling the gutter like it couldn't get enough innuendo to save its life. *Lord*, but he was a good-looking hunk of a man. A *huge* good-looking hunk of a man. Gwen usually went for skinny rocker boys with soulful eyes, bad hair, and worse personal baggage. She wasn't, by nature, an "I can fix him" girl, which meant those relationships tended to burn out fast and hard, but man, she had a hard time resisting the look.

Which was clearly because she had never met a look

like Bill Torben before. She would have rearranged her personal aesthetic to be nothing *but* six-foot-five mountain-men types, if she'd ever met anybody like him before. She had *badly* hoped he wouldn't get out of the chair and she would get to sit in his lap, which was even more forward than Gwen generally thought of herself as being, and she rarely wasted much time dilly-dallying with guys. They were either into her or not, and she preferred finding out up front.

She was pretty sure Bill was into her, but for the first time in her life, she felt very slightly hesitant about asking. It would be too disappointing if he wasn't. Maybe just this once, living in hope would be better than being crushed.

Besides, it looked like in order to save his festival, they were going to have to spend the next few days mostly in each other's company. If he wasn't into her *yet*, Gwen decided, she would by God do her best to make sure he was by the end of the weekend.

"All right," she said briskly. "You said your brothers knew about some music venues? Text them and see where's good. We'll start with their recommendations and go from there. Is there somewhere I can leave my guitar? I was going to check the sound from your stage, but it looks like we've got more important stuff to do right now. I'll do that in the morning."

As she spoke, Bill's phone began to ding and buzz with incoming text notifications, and he grimaced from the bones out. "That'll be my family just reading the update about how good ol' Bill blew it and booked the wrong talent. I don't even want to look at it." With a sigh, though, he took his phone out, shoulders bowed as he unlocked it and skimmed through texts.

Gwen's heart went out to him abruptly. He looked tired, like he was carrying too much weight, and she had the impulse to hug him and tell him everything was going to be all right. "Hey. Bill. Hey. Look at me."

He did, a hangdog expression in his brown eyes, and she shook her head. "If they're going to get to you, don't look at it right now. We're working on fixing it, which is clear from the update I sent out."

"Well, I can't just not respond," he said blankly. "They're expecting me to."

"As it turns out, you *can* just not respond. Ask me how I know." Gwen gave him an encouraging smile. "And if you can't get an answer out of your brothers about the music venues without dealing with the rest of their questions, then we'll figure it out without them. Online reviews are there for a reason. C'mon," she said with a tilt of her head toward the door. "Give me a place to store the guitar, and we'll blow this joint."

"You can leave it here, if that's okay? The door locks and I can give you a key." He gave his phone another guilty glance, but put it in his back pocket and went to the filing cabinet to take a key out of a drawer labeled K.

Gwen grinned as he handed it to her. "Subtle."

"You would be amazed at how my brothers can't remember K is for key," Bill said with a sigh. "Sometimes I think it *is* subtle." His phone buzzed again and he winced, reaching for it.

Gwen grabbed his hand. "Half an hour. Give me half

an hour to get you out of here and to a local jam session before you look at that."

"It's barely three in the afternoon," Bill protested. "There aren't going to be any jam sessions on at this hour."

"Oh ye of little faith." Gwen, keeping his huge hand in hers, pulled him toward the door. Bill slowed, but only enough to lock the door behind them. Then he came along willingly enough, although when she glanced back at him, he looked slightly befuddled. Apparently bossy rock stars didn't often come along and drag him out of his comfort zone.

Well, that was fair. Rock stars didn't usually come along and drag anybody out of their comfort zones, not literally. And Gwen might be overstating things a bit by calling herself a rock *star*, but dreams were for dreaming big with. Hand in giant hand with Bill Torben, she went back down the staff hall and out into the main pub, which was unexpectedly bright after the quiet dark office. A few more people had shown up, but nobody who seemed particularly interested in them, which was exactly what Bill needed right now. Gwen could practically feel guilt dragging his thoughts toward the phone he was bravely not looking at.

They almost made it out the door before hitting the first setback.

A good-looking man several years younger than Bill Torben, but clearly cut from the same cloth, came bounding—Gwen thought that was the right word, *bounding*—in through the main doors just as they were about to leave. Bill stopped dead, and the younger man's voice shot up in enthusiastic greeting. "*Bill!* There you are! Mom's going nuts because you're not answering the family chat. Dude, what the hell? We all got the email update but you didn't tell *us* first? Wha—"

"That's my fault," Gwen said firmly. She was forced to release Bill's hand to offer hers to the exuberant Torben brother, because this was very obviously one of Bill's brothers. "Gwen Booker, the accidental talent. Oh, I like that," she said mostly to herself.

"I'm Laurie." The younger Torben shook her hand automatically. He really did look a great deal like Bill, although not quite as tall or broad, and somewhat... *prettier*, Gwen decided. Not feminine by any stretch of the imagination, but his features were just slightly finer than his older brother's, and he wore his own sandy blonde hair long and loose. If she'd met him first, Gwen thought she might have thought Laurie Torben was the epitome of Hot Guy, but having met Bill, his younger brother looked slightly unfinished and a bit lacking to her eye. "*You're* the band we hired?"

"Well, I'm the lead singer, yeah. Gwen Booker," she repeated. "And it's my fault about not notifying your family first, sorry. I was helping Bill set up the email update we sent out and we got caught up in it instead of thinking to let you guys know first."

"You *really* don't look like a jazz singer."

Gwen laughed. "That's because I'm not. Which you know, if you read the email update."

"How the hell did you book *her* instead of Gwendolyn Brooker?" Laurie's gaze snapped from Gwen—

which felt dismissive and made her set her jaw—to Bill, who grimaced again.

"I wasn't paying enough attention." He shrugged. "That's it, really. I was in a hurry and trying to get it done—" He drew a sharp, deep breath through his nose, loud enough that Gwen glanced up to find him arranging his expression into a brief, determined, dismissive smile. "—and I screwed up. That's it."

"Man, that's not like you. You never drop the ball. It'll probably be okay." Laurie offered Gwen what he probably meant to be a devastatingly gorgeous grin. It sort of grated on her nerves. "You seem pretty cool."

"I am," she assured him with a brief smile of her own. "Hey, since we've got you here, do you have any recommendations on clubs or gig spaces in Renaissance? With the change in music style, we need to do some advertising at places that are looking for a rock concert, not an evening of jazz."

Laurie laughed. "Are you just going to let her take over your whole job, Bill?"

She watched another rigid grimace that almost passed for a smile cross the older Torben brother's face. "No. I've got it under control." He turned that same expression on Gwen, although she thought his brown eyes softened a bit. "I do have it under control. Thanks for your help, though."

Gwen took a breath to argue, then held it, studying the big man and his stiff shoulders and even stiffer smile. There was more going on here than she understood, and she had the sudden, distinct impression that insisting wasn't going to help. Or rather, it *would* help, in the sense that Bill clearly needed it, but it would undermine the *something else* that was happening right now. She put her hand on his forearm before realizing that was at least the second time she'd touched him without permission, but he didn't pull away and for a moment, neither did she. The muscles beneath her hand were strong and warm, and she gave his arm a little squeeze. "Okay then. Look, in that case, for my own sake, I'd still love to know about any clubs you can recommend, Laurie, and then I'm dying for a cup of coffee, so if either of you could point me toward the best local cafe…?"

"The Harlequin on Main and Fourth," Laurie said promptly. "They've got a good scene. And Moxie's on Quad Street is a dance club, but it has a lot of live music and brings people in all the time. And I'd love to take you out for coffee."

"That's all right," Bill said in a suddenly thunderous tone. "I can drop her at Candy's on my way into town. I've got some errands to run."

"Dude," Laurie said with great sincerity, "you've got an absolute shit ton of stuff to figure out in like no time, and if you don't answer the family chat Mom's going to go into cardiac arrest, so I don't know if you should be running errands."

Gwen watched with grim concern as the back of Bill's neck started to turn red, burning toward his ears in a very different flush of color than his earlier blushes had been. "Candy's would be great, assuming there's coffee there."

"Sure, let me bring you do—"

"I've got it, Laurie." Bill Torben's voice dropped into a rumble prit near indistinguishable from a growl. Hairs stood up on Gwen's arms, but it wasn't a fear response at all. Not at aaaalllll. Her whole body tightened with heat, and she felt a blush of her own crawling up her cheeks. She had all *kinds* of good ideas about how that rumble could rock her world, and she felt that she knew a thing or two about world-rocking in specific.

Laurie blinked rapidly, and while he didn't quite take a step back, he did lean back a little, visibly startled. "Jeez, okay, whatever. I've gotta go work on my baldric anyway. I'll see you later, man. Nice to meet you, Gwen." He edged past his brother and went into the pub, phone out and thumbs dancing over the screen. Gwen bet he was updating the family on having run into Bill, but there were more important questions to ask.

"Did he say…baldric?"

Bill sighed from what appeared to be the bottom of his soul, and on a man his size, that was a *big* sigh. "Yeah. It's a shoulder belt for a sword, like the Three Musketeers would use."

Gwen's mouth worked, trying to hold back a giggle. "Does your brother often need a belt to carry his sword in?"

Bill did a double-take at her so hard she thought she heard his neck pop before he gave a reluctant laugh. "God, I hope not. We already hear enough about his escapades. We'd never hear the end of that one. No, he's a re-enactor. He does Renaissance faires, specifically.

There's a huge one here every summer. Did you really want coffee?"

"I always want coffee." Gwen walked under Bill's arm as he pushed the door open for her. "Of course there's a huge Renaissance faire in a town called Renaissance. Which came first, the faire or the name?"

"The name, obviously. The town was founded in the 1870s. I don't think anybody was doing Ren faires then. But when they started to be a thing…" Bill sighed. "Yeah. Obviously there's a huge one in a town called Renaissance. It's actually how Thunder Bear Brewery got started. Mom and Dad were into the faire right away, and Dad started his own home brew to sell at it. It did really well, like, *really* well, and about five years later they built this place." He waved back at the building as they went into the parking lot. "The rest is history. I'm sorry about all this," he added. "I'll drop you off for coffee—"

"Aw." Gwen turned a hopeful gaze up at him as they reached her car, which was apparently parked next to his truck, a huge thing that managed to make Bill look regular-sized. "I was really hoping you'd come for coffee with me."

It was more than a little flattering to watch whatever resistance might have been in the big man just melt away into a soft smile. "Yeah," he said quietly. "Yeah, I'd like that."

CHAPTER 5

The *smart* thing to do was not go to coffee with Gwen. The smart thing to do was go figure out how to deal with the fiasco he'd instigated. But first off, Bill didn't want to do the smart thing, and second, even if he had, the hopeful look in her ice-blue eyes would have convinced him otherwise under basically any circumstances. He melted. He knew he was melting.

His bear looked at him curiously. *You're not melting.*

Trust me. I'm melting.

The bear examined him even more carefully, radiating dubiousness, but it didn't say anything else. That was helpful, because Bill could barely manage one conversation, never mind two, when Gwen was looking up at him with that sweet blue gaze. He managed to say, "Your truck or mine?" and was stunned when she gave a delighted squeal and bounced, clapping her hands together.

"Yours! I've never ridden in a monster truck before.

Oh, but wait. You're not going to kidnap me or anything, are you?"

The thought of running off into the woods with her forever, and not dealing with the real world at all ever again, briefly glowed in Bill's mind like it was the goal of all goals. His bear perked up again, eager for that endgame. But reality reasserted itself, and Bill said, "No," wryly. "Even if I tried, everybody in town knows who I am and I'd get turned in to my family before I managed to get you halfway kidnapped."

"Excellent." Gwen gave him a merry smile and went around to the passenger side of his truck, bouncing to see him over the hood. It was, he had to admit, a ridiculously big vehicle. Unfortunately for him, he'd once been forced to shift into a bear while in a Honda Civic, and ever since, the idea of a small car gave him the heebie jeebies.

His bear sent a sad image of itself stuffed into the Honda, fur and feet sticking out everywhere, through the windows, into the footwells, against the horn, which blared like a Fourth of July parade while it tried to cover its ears with its paws. It hadn't succeeded. So no more small cars for Bill. He just drove incredibly carefully with his stupidly huge truck. He unlocked the doors, nodded at Gwen, and grinned a bit as he watched her clamber up the chrome runner boards to climb in and sprawl against the leather seats. "You look like you belong in a monster truck."

"It's my viiiiibe, baby." Gwen did a hang-loose wobble with her hand and threw an arm across the back of the seats. "This is amazing. I think I can see

Denver from here. Also, are those ants on the ground, or children?" She made a show of looking out the window, peering at the parking lot asphalt.

Bill, who hadn't thought he could feel like laughing after running into Laurie, found himself chortling, at least. "It's not *that* high."

"You're starting from nine inches farther off the ground than I am in the first place," Gwen informed him. "Trust me, it *is* that high! Now, are we going for coffee or to check out the clubs your brother mentioned?"

"Uh." Bill felt his jaw fall open, and did his best to crank it back into place. "Uh?"

"Coffee, then," Gwen said decisively. "*Then* clubbing."

Bill, faintly, said, "But," and then decided that fate had thrown him a fast ball and he should do his best to catch it. Or run with it. Something like that. "Okay."

It was only a few minutes' drive to Candy's Coffee. It was Bill's favorite coffee shop in the area not just because the coffee was genuinely good, but because Candy, who was in her sixties and an old hippie at heart, had defied the city council and personally financed solar panels to cover her small parking lot with. The entire strip mall had eventually thrown in and now the parking lot was seventy percent covered by the panels, which provided all the power for the mall and put some back into the grid. Gwen said, "Oooh," in delight when she saw them. "That must keep the parking lot cooler in the summers, but doesn't it snow here? How do they keep them clear in the winter?"

"They've got self-powered heating elements in them," Bill said with a smile. "Melts the snow off."

"Oh, damn, that's clever! I love it!" Gwen swung out of the truck like she'd been in and out of monster trucks her whole life, and swaggered toward the coffee shop. It was definitely a swagger, too. Bill had never seen anybody move like that. Like a rock star. He trailed a few steps farther behind than necessary, admiring everything about that swagger. Her strong legs, her fine ass, the confident set of her shoulders, the way she tossed her hair...*everything*. God, he'd never met a woman as perfect as she was.

She stopped dead a couple steps inside Candy's, with its linoleum floors, brightly painted walls, and surprisingly cozy booths, then turned to him with an accusing look. "You said it was a *coffee* shop. You didn't tell me there was ice cream!"

Bill glanced beyond her at the two long freezers of home made ice cream that was Candy's other speciality, and back at Gwen. "You said you wanted coffee!"

"I didn't know ice cream was on the table!"

A sly grin crawled across his face. "I think you should eat it out of a bowl."

Gwen laughed out loud. "Oh my God, you're one of those. A bad jokes dude."

His eyebrows rose. "Aren't they usually called 'dad jokes?'"

"They are." Gwen ordered an ice cream sundae that he knew would be as big as her face, and a coffee almost equal in size. "I don't like that phrase, though. There's already this whole idea in society that women aren't funny, and I think calling those silly, easy quips 'dad jokes' plays into that. Everybody makes them."

"Whoa. I never thought of it like that." He followed her to a table, sitting down as they waited for their orders to be called. "Right. No more dad jokes, just bad jokes."

She flashed a smile. "My hero. So, look, do you—" She broke off as their coffee orders were called. "Wow. Fast. Hang on."

"I can get them!" Bill rose swiftly, feeling like he should be a proper gentleman and carry things. Gwen gestured like 'be my guest,' and he went to the counter, getting the tray that held his reasonable-sized coffee, and Gwen's gigantic sundae and mocha. He came back to the table, placing them in front of the appropriate seats, and Gwen's eyes widened.

"I didn't know I was ordering the Mount Everest of ice cream sundaes. Are you sure you didn't mix ours up?"

"*I*," Bill emphasized, "*know* better than to order a sundae called an 'Avalanche.'"

"You know you're going to have to help me eat this."

Bill grinned. "That's why I didn't order my own, yeah. You have excellent taste in ice cream, by the way." She'd ordered a five-scooper with dark chocolate, raspberry, and cherry ice creams, plus Candy's own hot fudge and raspberry coulis toppings, whipped cream, and no fewer than five cherries on top.

"Thank you. Please proceed to be impressed with

how much of this I'll be able to eat." Gwen dug in and groaned with delight at her first bite. "Oh my God, that's really good…everything. Ice cream. Most chocolate ice cream is lacking, but that's amazing. And the hot fudge!"

"I know," Bill said, pleased, as if he was personally responsible for the concoction. "Candy's been running this place for forty years and she wins best ice cream competitions all over the world. The coffee's also really good." He took a sip of his own, watching Gwen enjoy her ice cream with a smile.

She got more than halfway through the huge sundae before nodding at him. "Okay, you can help now. What a gentleman, waiting for me to gorge."

Bill laughed. "That's not how I would have put it!"

"Because you're a gentleman," she said with a sage nod. "So do you want to talk about it?"

He froze with a spoon halfway to the sundae. "Talk about…?"

Gwen waved her own spoon in the general direction of the brewpub. "The whole thing with your family and the pub. There's clearly a lot going on there for you on a, like, personal level. Who better to unburden yourself to than some random rock chick who's gonna be gone at the end of the weekend?"

A crash of real dismay smashed through Bill's chest, making his hand tremble until the spoon actually wobbled. He put it down, not wanting to look—weak, he thought, and momentarily closed his eyes. That was exactly what Gwen was talking about, even if she didn't exactly know it. And in her case, it was the idea that she would be gone in a few days that he could barely stand to imagine. A little part of him protested that she couldn't just up and leave! He'd just found her! She was his fated mate!

But she was also a person with a career of her own, and throwing it all away to watch him struggle with the family business was certainly not on her list of things to do. Even if it suddenly was somehow on that list, Bill would have to be a world-class jackass to keep her from her own dreams.

World-class bear, his bear rumbled reassuringly. *Not jackass.*

A breath of air escaped him, nowhere near a laugh, but flavored like one. *Yeah, buddy. A world-class bear.* Which was another thing he'd have to explain at some point.

Maybe not now, though. Not with those pale blue eyes studying him with a concern Bill wouldn't expect from a stranger.

Not a stranger, his bear said, still rumbling and reassuring. *Our mate.*

Still a stranger, Bill argued, but without heat. Aloud, uncertainly, he said, "Look, none of it's your problem, and I'm sure you don't really want to hear about a ton of family politics."

Gwen put her hand on top of his. Her fingers were cold from gripping a metal spoon that had been diving into ice cream, but the coolness felt good, and he had a sudden, deeply inappropriate thought about where else those cool fingers might feel good. Fortunately, she said, "I actually do. I saw how you were holding back a couple of times at things your brother said, and we only talked to him for about two minutes. There's clearly a *lot* going on there. Unburden yourself. That crack he made about me taking over your job, that landed. How come?"

A burst of rough, unhappy laughter erupted from Bill's chest so hard it startled him. "Because I'd love for somebody to take over. Or at least fucking help!"

Horror washed through him as he realized how angry he'd sounded, but before he could apologize, Gwen took a deep breath and let it out on a soft, "And there we have it."

"I didn't mean you!" Bill blurted, mortified, and got the softest, kindest smile he could imagine in return.

"No, obviously, of course you didn't. But seriously, you've got the vibe of a guy who's been carrying it all alone for way too long, and nobody's noticing. I know I'm a flash in the pan in your life, but I'm noticing, okay? So what's the deal? Parents started the business, you're the oldest, so it falls to you to continue it whether you want to or not?"

"It's not even that I don't want to!" Bill slumped, then lifted the spoon again and began fiddling at the edge of a scoop of ice cream, not really sure he should eat some of her sundae while also unburdening himself to Gwen's sympathetic shoulder. It seemed rude, some-how. "Mom and Dad are retired, move-to-Arizona-live-the-good-life retired, and after running the place for a few years, I can't blame them. But Laurie and Jon have no idea how much work it is, and it doesn't matter how often I ask them to help out. They'll do the one thing I ask, and that's it. They run the faire stuff," he admitted to the sundae. "But the rest of it, it's all on me. And we're losing business," he said even more quietly. "I'd hire an assistant manager, but I don't have the budget. So instead, I screw up and hire Gwen Booker, rock star, instead of Gwendolyn Brooker for our jazz festival opener. And you," he said, lifting his gaze, "let it go earlier. When I said I had everything under control. Why'd you do that?"

Her gorgeous eyes widened a bit. "Your brother wanted to tease you, and you were having a bad moment, and I thought arguing would give him more ammunition for a fight you didn't need."

A little flare of something happened in Bill's heart, like a cut was healing. "Are you always this empathetic?"

"Nah. Only toward huge, gorgeous guys who look at me like I'm a mix of their hottest dream and worst nightmare." Gwen laughed as Bill felt dismay slide over his face. "Oh, come on, big man. Am I wrong?"

"Well—no—but—" Bill spluttered, then shoved a big bite of ice cream into his mouth so he had time to come up with a decent response. He hadn't thought he'd been so obvious about either of those things, but from Gwen's grin, he clearly had been. When the ice cream was gone, he sighed. "Sorry."

"For what? Thinking I'm hot? Under the circumstances I get why I'm your worst nightmare, but I've got no problems with being your hottest dream, too. Seriously, man," she added more quietly. "Your brother's kind of a brat, but have you sat the family down and told them how much you need help?" She paused, examining his expression, then nodded sympathetically. "Yeah, I didn't think so. Arright, well, look, I'm not going to be the rando who comes into your life and pushes you around, then leaves you wondering what happened to that manic pixie dream girl. But if you'll let me, I *will* try to help you get through this weekend successfully."

"*Why?*"

"Because it's good for me, too?"

That was hard to argue with. Bill chuckled and fiddled with another bite of ice cream before finally meeting Gwen's eyes and nodding. "All right. Yeah, I'll take your help. Thank you, Gwen Booker, Accidental Talent."

CHAPTER 6

"Well, you're welcome, Bill Torben..." Gwen ran out of things to say, because 'dude I'd like to climb like a tree' didn't really fit into the same scansion as 'Accidental Talent' did. Eventually, feeling silly for having tried to echo him, she just said, "You're welcome," again, and smiled.

It was true, as far as it went. She wanted to help him get the weekend sorted out because it was good for her and her band. But more than that, she knew what it was like to feel like you were the only one keeping everything afloat, while everyone around you went along like everything was great. It was lonely and exhausting and in her experience, ended *incredibly* badly. Even if she could *only* help for a weekend—and for some reason that thought gave her a funny little pang in the heart—she could at *least* help for the weekend. Maybe it would be enough. "How long have you been in charge?"

"About five years now, I guess." Bill said it like a man who could give it to her in days, hours, and minutes, but was trying to restrain himself. "My second brother, Steve, he used to help a lot, but he moved away a few years ago and it's basically been me ever since." He glanced at the almost-finished sundae between them, looked embarrassed, and pushed it a few inches back toward her. "I've eaten all your ice cream."

Gwen laughed and shook her head. "I ate all I could. Go ahead and finish it."

"I can't. It's yours." He hesitated. "But I could eat all but the last bite."

Gwen accidentally said, "Aww," right out loud, and for the third time since she'd met him, Bill Torben blushed. She loved that he blushed easily. It made her want to suggest increasingly blush-inducing things, to see if he would spontaneously combust, or better yet, take her up on some of those things. Instead she promised, "I'll eat the last bite," and watched him sheepishly eat everything but. Then she dug into the bowl with her spoon, impressed he'd managed to leave her some hot fudge in the bottom, and savored the last bite with a happy sigh. "Okay, that was worth it. Thanks for sharing it with me."

"Anything else you want to share?"

Gwen looked up with a delighted grin, and Bill's ears went scarlet. "I mean, I just kind of unburdened myself on you. Do you have anything you need to talk about?"

"You mean like, am I afraid I'm wasting my best

years on trying to crack the airwaves as a rock star in a world where the radio only carries pop and hip hop? Do I wonder how I'm going to pay next month's bills without another gig scheduled? Whether I should throw it all in for the van life, because at least that way I don't have to worry about rent? Nah," Gwen said with a shake of her head. "No, I'm good, thanks."

"I could never do it," Bill said almost before she'd finished trying to downplay her own stresses. "It's hard enough running the pub, and it's got a forty year history of success behind it. Trying to make it in a creative field where you don't have any control over whether people find your work, or like it, or buy it instead of pirating it? How *do* you do it?"

The questions and the insight actually took Gwen's breath away, leaving her gazing at the big man with her lips parted and a rush of astonishment wiping out all the words in her mind. When she was finally able to speak, she landed on the last part of what he'd said, because, "Nobody except artists ever thinks about digital piracy and how it affects them. How do you even know that's a problem?"

Bill looked sheepish. "You remember those old warnings they used to show before movies? 'You wouldn't steal a car?' The first time I saw them I didn't even know what digital piracy was, so I looked it up and found out it's all kind of a big mess, especially for smaller artists. Not that it's cool to pirate a big movie or something, but I get the idea that musicians, like you, or writers, or people who draw or whatever, that maybe your numbers are affected enough by that kind of stuff to really be the line between making it or not."

"You're really right." Gwen gave him a crooked grin. "Like, *really* right. I know a lot of artsy types, and it's a real problem, like the difference between albums being made or not, or sequels getting published, or comics getting finished. All kinds of things. And I don't know how I do it," she admitted. "Sometimes just by not thinking about any of it, because if I think about the odds I'll lose my mind."

"'Never tell me the odds,' eh?"

"Hah! Yeah. Yeah, I guess so."

"So does that mean you're living the van life?"

"Aaaaah!" Gwen threw her head back, rolling her eyes at the ceiling, then smiled ruefully at Bill. "No, not quite yet, although sometimes I honestly think it'd be easier. Just stay on the road all the time, go from gig to gig. Except there aren't always enough gigs, so I gotta keep the day job."

His eyebrows rose and he looked her as up-and-down as he could, given that she was sitting across a table from him and so at least half of her body was hidden from his view. "You have a day job?"

Gwen, deadpan, said, "I work at an ice cream shop," and Bill's eyes flew open. She laughed. "No, it's worse than that. I'm a receptionist."

"For a music company?" Bill's voice rose, and Gwen couldn't help another snicker.

"You'd think, wouldn't you? No, you've got to look at this." She took her driver's license out, pushing it across the table. "I think of that as 'Gwen, Playing Human.'"

"You're definitely already human," he said absently, but picked up the card to examine the little picture of her with her dark hair tied neatly back, her makeup neutral and not at all eye-catching, and wearing a pink blouse with a Peter Pan collar. "Holy sh—I mean, uh, you look like a different person."

"'Day Job Gwen,'" she agreed, taking the license back. "About the only thing that's recognizable are my freaky pale eyes. I look like they took a vacation in Antarctica."

"They're perfect rock star eyes," Bill said a little vehemently. "Able to cut right through your soul. Perfect."

"Oh." A stupid little grin pulled at her mouth. "Oh. Thanks. That's. Gosh. Thanks. Maybe the nicest thing anybody's ever said about them. I always thought they looked freezer-burned. Like I should be able to shoot ice beams out of them." She turned her head and squinted dramatically, pretending she was spraying ice from her eyes and going *pew crackle pew pew* for the sound effects.

"That would be *so cool*," Bill said, and when she looked at him, spread his hands and smiled. "Who doesn't like superheroes?" Or other people with unusual gifts, like turning into grizzly bears. He wondered how Gwen was going to react to that.

"Well, I'm afraid my only real superpower is playing a mean riff on the guitar, and hitting the high notes every time. Seriously, though, thanks." Gwen pushed the empty ice cream bowl to the middle of the table and finished her coffee. "So should we go check out these venues?"

"I dunno. Are you gonna play for me?" Bill smiled as they stood and she glanced at him in surprise. "Well, it seems like I should have some idea of what you sound like, since I hired you for the festival, right?"

She clicked her tongue. "Should have brought my guitar, then. Maybe later. Do you have an opening act, or is it just me and the girls?"

Bill made a face as they headed out of the ice cream parlor/coffee shop. "No opening act. We used to have one, back when things were going better, but people didn't show up until the main event anyway, so I let it go a couple of years ago. And I've been worried about that," he admitted. "Although it probably wouldn't have been great to book a jazz act and then have a rock band follow it."

"So what's the deal with the numbers falling?" Gwen swung up into his truck like a pro, buckling in as she asked questions.

"I'm not sure," Bill said with a wince. "Things were fine up until Mom and Dad retired, and..." A gulf of uncertainty opened in his chest, and he found himself saying, "I'm afraid I'm just not any good at this. That it's me, somehow. They did so well for so long, and I'm just trying to keep it going for them, but..."

"For them?" Gwen's voice softened, like the question was sharp enough on its own.

He glanced at her, seeing kindness in those cool

blue eyes of hers, and exhaled. "Steve went off and built his own place in upstate New York. Part of me is crazy envious, but..." He shook his head. "I don't want to leave Renaissance. I love it here. I even love the pub. I just don't know how to keep it going. I used to actually do the brewing, you know? Developing a new IPA was one of my favorite things to do. But there's not much time for that anymore."

"What's your audience like?" Gwen laughed at herself. "I mean, your clientele. Young, old, in between?"

"Pretty old, honestly. Closer to Mom and Dad's ages than ours. Mine, I mean. You're probably about twenty-seven."

"Thirty-five. How old are you?"

"Thirty-eight next month. So we're not that far apart. But a lot of the clientele's in their sixties."

"So on one hand, maybe retired, a lot of free time to come hang at the pub. On the other hand, maybe not looking for a really loud night with hundreds of strangers. Maybe you secretly hired me on purpose. Maybe your subconscious is telling you it's time to rebrand."

Bill threw a genuinely startled look her way as he turned down Fourth Street toward the Harlequin, the place Laurie had recommended. "Rebrand? No, I couldn't, it'd kill Mom and Dad."

"Yeah? Have they told you that? 'Hey, Bill, never rebrand the Thunder Bear Brewpub. It would kill us.'"

He squinted at her. "You're kind of..."

Gwen smiled sunnily at him, her dark wine rock

star lipstick at odds with the sparkling expression. "Abrupt? To the point? Blunt? An asshole?"

"I wasn't going to say that!"

She cackled, letting it turn into a full wheezing laugh. "Probably not, because you seem like a pretty decent guy, but it's possible I'm a bit of an asshole sometimes. I'm sorry. It's just...have you ever seen *While You Were Sleeping?*"

"Um. No?"

"It's an old Sandra Bullock romcom. Top ten desert island movie for me. Point is, the hero is a guy who's supposed to inherit the family business, but he doesn't want to, and he's afraid to talk to his dad about it because he doesn't want to hurt the old man's feelings. I watched it when I was really young, and I kind of decided I'd try to just go ahead and have the hard conversations in my life, because putting them off doesn't seem to help anybody very much."

"Wow. How's that worked out for you?" He pulled them into the Harlequin's parking lot. He hadn't been in there since he was a teenager pretending to be a little older than he was, but the colorfully-painted harlequin mask that gave the club its name still looked fresh and new where it rose partway above the building's roof, and the club's name, outlined in bright lights, had every bulb in place, shining merrily. It was all well-cared-for, which gave him a sense of satisfaction.

Gwen wobbled a hand as they parked. "Well, it's cut a lot of bad relationships short, anyway. That's something."

His bear roused, offended. *Who's been bad to our mate? We'll swat them!*

Bill sort of felt the same way, although he didn't make the offer out loud. Instead he said, "It sounds terrifying," which was a little more honest than he'd intended to be.

"It is, at first. Although I guess it helps if you start when you're about twelve." She smiled at him, then laughed as he gestured for her to wait, got out of the truck, went around, opened the door, and offered her a hand down. "What a gentleman. The thing is, we make things worse in our heads than they are a lot of the time, and if it turns out they really *are* that bad? At least we've got more information. What's the absolute worst that could happen if you told your folks you wanted to rebrand?"

"I don't think it would actually kill them," Bill conceded. "I guess…they'd be disappointed, or hurt, or angry. I guess that's what I'm worried about."

"And how do you think they'd feel knowing you're miserable with things the way they are?"

Bill's jaw dropped open. "I'm not miserable!" A stab of guilt shot through him as he protested, though. Maybe he was unhappier than he could even let himself admit.

It was too bad it took his fated mate showing up to make him realize that. He would have preferred to be solid and reliable as a rock for her, not struggling to find his own path. He felt the dismay growing in his chest and on his face, and wondered how he could possibly be a good mate to a woman who seemed to have her act totally together, when he couldn't even admit to himself he was unhappy.

"Hey." Gwen put her hand on his arm, encouraging him to look down at her. She smiled when he met her eyes, and tilted her head toward the Harlequin. "Best way I know to blow off a little angst is through rock and roll, baby. Let's go check it out."

CHAPTER 7

Gwen *liked* Bill Torben. She'd only known him a couple of hours, but he was such a big solid lunk of a guy who clearly cared deeply about his family and their business. She wanted him to be able to have his cake and eat it too, and never mind that she wouldn't hate being the cake that was being eaten. Which was a mess of a metaphor, but that didn't matter.

What mattered was the resignation and sadness in the big man's dark eyes, and her desire to do something about it. He'd obviously been shocked at her probably-too-blunt assessment that he was miserable, but Gwen was pretty sure she wasn't wrong.

She was *absolutely* sure she was right about music being a balm for the soul, though. "I am," she confessed as they went into the club, "assuming you *like* rock music. Oh, this is nice."

The Harlequin kept its theme going from the enormous, Carnival-bright painted mask on the sign outside to its interior, which was done in reds and golds with white accents, making it vivid and almost bright even with the lights down low. A variety of seating scattered through the space, from a small set of tiered, stadium-style theatre seats to round couches around tables, and other individual or small chairs and sofas. The flooring had raised areas, and there was an open upstairs with metal railing at about chest-height. Gwen bet it kept drunk people from falling downstairs.

There was a real stage setup at the far end, and the whole space was clearly oriented to focus on that. It had theatrical lights, curtains, a microphone and drum set, and a couple of stools for musicians to use. There was a glimpse of a just-barely-visible backstage area, too, and from the way the back of the building was structured, Gwen thought there were probably dressing rooms and maybe even enough space for setting up back there. Impressed, she said, "This is the real deal. How do you not come here?" before shaking her head. "Silly question. You're busy running the pub."

"And before I was running it I was..." Bill shrugged. "I did a lot around the place."

Gwen bet that meant he'd been running it unofficially for quite a while before he'd started doing it officially. "Well, we're just going to have to figure out some way to make sure you get time of your own, big man. You need down time, too, you know." Ideally spent with her, except she would be gone after the weekend. Gwen didn't mind fly-by-night affairs, but Bill Torben didn't seem like the kind of guy who went for one night stands. Besides, for some reason the idea made her heart ache a little. Even though she'd just met the guy, it was like the idea of stealing just a few days with him wouldn't ever be enough. Which was ridiculous, but hearts were capricious things. Gwen shook herself, pushing the thoughts away to ask, "*Do* you like rock music?"

"I don't know any new rock," Bill admitted sheepishly. "I don't hear much of it on the radio."

"No, like I said, it's all pop and hiphop, or at least, a lot of it is. But that implies you know older stuff? And like it?" Gwen asked hopefully.

He grinned. "Yeah. That's me, a wannabe metalhead."

Gwen laughed. "Good. Gonna have to grow your hair out to really thrash it, but we'll work with what we've got." Someone came out on stage, obviously not paying attention to the relatively small number of people scattered through the club, and sat down with their back half to the audience, tuning a guitar and singing under their breath. "Come on, let's go ask if they know who the manager is." She scurried up to the stage, leaning on it in the musician's eyeline until they finished what they were doing and turned to look at her.

They were cute: androgynous, shaggy hair, large eyes, shapeless clothes, and held the guitar like they were comfortable with it. Gwen couldn't help smiling a little wistfully. She would have liked to have spent her own teen years figuring herself out like that, hiding in floppy clothes and wrapped around a guitar. "Hi! I'm Gw—"

"Gwen Booker," the musician whispered, their eyes getting considerably larger. "Holy shit, you're *Gwen Booker*! From the Sixty Pix, right? The lead singer? You're—what are *you* doing here?"

A thrill broke from Gwen's throat in a laugh that turned into a beaming smile. She didn't get recognized all that often, and it was still incredibly cool to her when she did. She shot a quick glance at Bill, who looked a bit starstruck himself, just because somebody had recognized her. Still beaming, Gwen turned back to the musician. "Yeah, that's me. I'm playing at the Thunder Bear Brewpub this weekend. What's your name?"

"Ripley. I'm Ripley." Their voice squeaked and they stood up, blushing. "Holy crap, I can't believe I'm talking to *Gwen Booker*!"

"Hey, Ripley." Gwen felt like her grin was going to split her face as she nodded at the guitar. "You been playing long?"

Ripley looked at the guitar in their hands like they'd never seen it before, although they were holding its neck with a throttlingly tight grip. "Oh. No. I mean, yes, but no? Not, like, not long enough to be *good* like you are."

Gwen lifted her chin, a little encouraging action. "Will you play something for me?"

Ripley, faintly, said, "Oh my God," and sat on their stool again like someone had cut their strings. "Me? Really? For you?"

"Yeah! I'd love to hear you!" Gwen took a couple steps back, spreading her hands, hoping it would encourage Ripley, who ducked their head over the guitar and audibly hyperventilated for a few seconds. Then they nodded and loosened their grip on the guitar, shook their shoulders, and, head still ducked, began to play.

It only took a few notes for Gwen to recognize the song as one of her own. She couldn't help laughing, and with a quick, sort-of apologetic glance at Bill, vaulted up on the stage and went to tap the microphone. It wasn't on, but she grabbed it anyway, theatrically, and when Ripley looked up with a gulp, Gwen nodded encouragingly at them. They lost their fingering for a moment, but she waited, and after another couple measures, they found it again, and took the intro of the song with more confidence. Gwen waited for her cue, lifting the mic to her mouth, and belted it out like she was playing for a crowd.

Ripley's eyes widened further and a smile leaped across their face. Before Gwen reached the end of the second line, the guitarist's confidence had soared, fingers dancing across the strings like they'd been playing with Gwen their whole life. By the end of the verse, Gwen was forehead to forehead with Ripley, both of them singing their hearts out as they grinned wildly at each other.

Halfway through the chorus, the mic turned on. Gwen's voice boomed across the club and she laughed into the microphone, pulling it a little farther away from her mouth now that it was live, and took half a step back from Ripley so the guitar's sound wouldn't distort. The crowd, such as it was at mid-afternoon, all came up to stand at the stage's edge, clapping and dancing and cheering. Bill stood thunderstruck in the middle of it, gazing up at Gwen like he'd just seen a star ignite. By then they clearly had to finish the song, so she and Ripley did, ending with a laugh and a bow first toward each other, then toward the little audience they'd gathered. Gwen, into the mic, said, "I'm sure you're all wondering why I've called you here today," and got another laugh. "Is there a manager in the house?"

"Yeah." A slender man whom Gwen would call tall if he hadn't been standing next to Bill, waved. He was silver-haired, a little craggy, dressed in soft clothing and bright colors, like he'd been a music producer in the 80s and never got over dressing like one. "I'm Mike Piccolo, and you're Gwen Booker. That was terrific. And I see you've met our resident genius, Ripley. What are you doing in town, Ms. Booker?"

Gwen went over to crouch at the edge of the stage and offered her hand to the manager. "I'm playing at the Thunder Bear this weekend, but I thought I'd come check out the local scene. Nice to meet you, Mr. Piccolo."

"Call me Mike, Mr. Piccolo is my father, et cetera," Piccolo said easily. "If you've got any spare time and want to come play the Harlequin, Ms. Booker…"

"Well, now." Gwen smiled and stood so she could put the mic back in its stand, then returned to the edge of the stage to hop down. Instead, Bill stepped forward, raising his hands.

Gwen could think of a list of people she would let

help her down from a stage by putting their hands on her waist and lifting her to the floor, and up until that very moment, that list had had exactly zero people on it. But Bill Torben's big hands slid around her waist with absolute confidence, and she had no fear at all as he moved her effortlessly to the floor. She ended up with her hand against his chest, somehow. He was warm and huge and she felt completely safe, looking up into his eyes. They crinkled a little with a smile, fine lines around them, and for a heart-stopping moment Gwen thought—hoped!—he was going to kiss her.

Instead he let her go and stepped back, expression sheepish again. Gwen wanted to heap reassurances on him: that had not only been okay, it had been *wonderful* and she wanted him to do it again and again and again. And also to see how many other circumstances he could lift her so easily in.

Possibly, though, right now when she was trying to make a professional connection was *not* the time for those experiments. Which Bill clearly recognized, faster than she had.

Either that or he wasn't interested in her at all and had only been doing her a favor, but with the lingering warmth of his hands on her waist and the memory of the softness in his eyes, Gwen didn't think that was the case. She smiled at him, trying not to look twitterpated, then firmly told herself to get her head in the game and turned to the Harlequin's manager. "I'd love to play here," she told him. "The acoustics are great. But we're in a bit of a pickle over at the bar. Can I buy you a drink and explain?"

Piccolo chuckled. "It's my gin joint. Drinks are on me. Bill," he said pleasantly to that man. "Haven't seen your parents around in a while. They doing okay?"

"They moved to Arizona," Bill said with a smile. "They're driving up for the festival, though. Should be here in a few hours. I'll let them know you asked after them. Gwen, I'll let you—"

"Don't be silly," Gwen interrupted. "It's your pickle we're in." She explained the mis-booking as they sat and Piccolo called for drinks, finishing with, "So we're looking for some quick and dirty ways to round up an audience for the pub this weekend, because I have many talents, but jazz music isn't one of them."

"When do you start there?" Piccolo's eyebrows drew down thoughtfully.

Gwen cast a glance at Bill, as if she didn't know the answer herself. "Tomorrow. It's a Friday and Saturday night gig."

"Got plans tonight? We don't usually have live music booked on Thursdays, but we do have an active chat group and if we put the word out I expect we could get a decent crowd tonight that would help spread the word for the weekend."

"If you don't mind just me and my guitar," Gwen said, making a face. "The band comes in tomorrow."

Piccolo flashed a grin that made him look twenty years younger. "Pretty sure Ripley up there knows every piece of music you've ever done, and there are some local drummers who won't put you to shame, if you want a backbeat. Now, I'm not talking about a paying gig, here," he added warningly.

Bill made a protesting sound. "Come on, Gwen Booker is a known commodity—"

"No, it's fine," Gwen interrupted. "Normally, no way, I don't get paid in exposure, people *die* of exposure, but in this particular case, let's look at it like a local pick-up gig where I just happened to show up and ask if I could get up on stage with the house band. Which, let's face it, isn't all that far from true."

"You're completely independent, aren't you?" Piccolo asked. "No record label, no manager?"

Gwen hesitated. "Yeah. I had some bad industry experiences early on and I thought I was better off avoiding the system, honestly." She felt, more than saw, Bill puff up a little at her side, as if he'd protect her from anything, even her own past. She smiled at him, and he returned the expression, although he still had that protective aura.

Usually, Gwen thought, that would annoy her. But somehow it was kind of charming from Bill Torben. Maybe because he just seemed like such a decent guy. Impulsively, she said, "You'll come to the gig tonight, right?" to him. "You know, so you have an idea of what you're getting into?"

Sheer alarm crossed his face. "Me? At a dance club? I don't fit in." He made a gesture at himself, like he was indicating his size, if nothing else. "And I can't dance."

Gwen absolutely couldn't help it. She *knew* her grin went sly, and she put on a deliberately sultry tone. "That's all right, big man. I like to be watched."

CHAPTER 8

Gwen Booker was going to be the death of him. Bill blushed *again*. He hadn't blushed this much since he was a teenager and had a crush on a girl whose name he couldn't even remember right now. She'd been the center of his world, at the time, and he bet she was still a terrific human being, but she couldn't possibly hold a candle to Gwen. To his *mate*. Who said lascivious things *right in front of other people*. He made a little strangled sound and Gwen laughed, putting her hand over his.

Her hands were small, but not smooth. Calloused, especially the fingertips, with little dented ridges from guitar strings. A shiver ran through him at the thought of those slightly rough fingertips stroking over his body, and his blush turned even hotter. He tried to sound normal as he said, "Then I'll just watch."

If the way Mike Piccolo tried to hide a laugh was any indication, he'd sounded like a horny teenage boy instead.

Gwen, still with her wicked grin, touched the tip of her tongue to the middle of her upper lip, and Bill thanked God he was sitting down, because the way his jeans suddenly got very uncomfortable made it clear that anybody who happened to glance at his crotch would see his interest was, uh, aroused. Then, as if she hadn't just given him an incredible hard-on, Gwen turned a cheerful smile back to Mike. "So what time tonight? Would Ripley want to make up a set list? That way they can be sure to pick stuff they're comfortable with playing."

Mike glanced at his phone, tapping his fingers against it before saying, "Eight o'clock, for a ninety minute set? I'd like to say nine, because it picks up here around then for a couple hours, but an early gig might get people in sooner, and I don't know what the rest of your schedule is like."

"The rest of the crew gets in around two tomorrow. Early enough to set up and test the acoustics at the pub without disturbing many patrons." Gwen cast another glance at Bill like she was checking to see if that lined up with his expectations, and he nodded.

"People start showing up for the Oktoberfest weekend around two," he said. "More come in after five, obviously, but yeah, that'll be fine."

Gwen beamed at him, and a warm happy flush ran through him. Not a blush, this time. Just a feeling of contentment. His mate was smiling at him, and all was right with the world.

Except all *wasn't* right with the world. He still had a festival weekend to pull off at a failing pub with the wrong entertainment, never mind trying to explain everything to his family. At least they'd stopped texting: his phone hadn't buzzed in a while.

Humans, his bear said, exasperated. *You worry too much.*

On one hand, he thought his bear was probably right. On the other, it wasn't the one trying to balance the books every month.

"So!" Gwen turned back to Mike. "Tell you what, I'll show up around seven-thirty, help set up, meet the crew, rub elbows a little, whatever you need. We'll hit the stage probably around eight-fifteen, just start to warm things up, and we'll call eight-thirty the start time, and play until ten. Hopefully that'll catch enough people to get some blood flowing and we'll draw a decent crowd to the pub over the weekend."

"You don't have to help set up," Mike said, but Gwen shook her head.

"Oh, but I do. Even if I just run a couple cables somewhere, it goes a long way toward smoothing things out and making sure people don't think I'm too big for my britches. If I'm gonna drop in like this, yeah, I'll put in the tech work too. So is seven-thirty good?"

"Sounds great." Mike offered Gwen a hand, and they shook before Mike tilted his head toward Ripley. "You want to ask them to make the set list?"

Gwen's grin lit up the whole room. "I'd love to." She bounced out of her chair and went back to the stage, leaning on it as she spoke to the young guitarist.

Mike watched her, then turned his attention to Bill. "You have no idea who you booked there, do you?"

"Um." Bill spread his hands, embarrassed.

"She would've been Joan Jett, in a different generation. Rock's hard to break through with these days. She's this far," Mike held up his fingers a centimeter apart, "from that big break anyway. Real underground following. Won't sell tickets through any of the big vendors, though, and hasn't signed with a label since they tried to make her into Britney."

"Gwen?" Bill turned to look at the woman leaning on the stage, somewhere between *of course* and *no way*, emotionally. "She doesn't look like a Britney type."

"No. She was famous as a kid star, but when she turned eighteen and they wanted to market her as the next pop princess, they couldn't get her to fit in the box. She put out an album so bad it's legendary." Mike chuckled. "It got her a lot of fans, in fact. They figured she couldn't have made an album that bad accidentally. But the label dumped her and she went dark, and has been on her own since. I would've killed to sign somebody like her when I was a producer."

"A kid star?" Bill glanced toward the stage again, shaking his head. "I don't remember any Gwen Booker, but I didn't pay much attention to music even when I was a kid. So wait a minute, you mean she's working as a secretary and thinking about the van life because she had too many principles to play ball with a label?" Bill wasn't certain he'd had all that many preconceived notions about Gwen in the couple hours he'd known her, but he found he was having to rearrange some anyway. "I figured she was..."

"Working as close to the top as she was ever going

to get? Nah. She could've been Pink, if she'd been able to play the game a little better. Or been willing to," Mike said. "I'm not sure she wasn't *able* to. Like I said, you have to know exactly what you're doing to put out an album that bad. I'd love to talk to her about it, but I'm not sure it's something she wants to discuss. She changed her name and disappeared after that album, so you had to actually be watching and paying attention to realize she's the same woman. Either way, you landed on your feet, Bill. If you were going to screw up a booking, getting Gwen Booker and the Sixty Pix was about the best you possibly could have done. This place will be packed tonight. Speaking of which." He rose. "I should go hit the mailing lists and the chat rooms and let them know about our special guest star tonight. I'll see you later?"

"Apparently I'll be watching," Bill said absently, and just barely managed not to blush again as Mike cackled.

"You'll like what you see," he predicted, and headed over to shake hands with Gwen, then went off to his own business. Bill waited where he was, feeling large and out of place in a club space clearly meant for lithe young things. He was neither lithe nor young anymore, although he knew he wasn't really that old. He just felt old sometimes, and remembered from his own youth how adults in their late thirties had looked *ancient* to him.

Gwen, though. She fit into this space. Apparently she'd fit into it her whole life, although he couldn't for the life of him place her as any teen or kid star he remembered. Regardless, she wasn't that much younger than he was. Maybe it was all a mindset. His was old and boring and staid, and hers was vibrant and young and challenging.

He would make a *terrible* mate for someone like Gwen.

Don't be silly, his bear said. *You're exactly what she needs. And she's what you need.*

I'm not sure, Bill replied. It wasn't that he doubted the mate bond. It was more that he couldn't see how this one would work. He had a local business to run, and Gwen was apparently bordering on being a breakout rock star. Those two things just didn't seem to fit together, to him.

It'll work out, his bear promised him, and Bill, who had a lot of other things to worry about, sighed quietly and for the moment decided to just try to trust the bear, and the power of fate. Gwen was still chatting with Ripley, and it gave him a moment to watch her without any other agenda. The way she leaned on the stage gave him an exceptionally nice view of her rear end, particularly of a tear in her jeans across the bottom of her left cheek. There was no sign of panties, although he assumed that meant they were high cut, rather than she wasn't wearing any. He'd always assumed wearing jeans without underwear must be uncomfortable for women, with the riding up he figured the denim would do. He'd also never asked.

You could ask Gwen, his bear said brightly.

Bill made a face. *Maybe when I've known her for more than two hours.*

Hmph. Two hours, two years, it won't matter. She's your mate. She'll tell you.

Maybe, Bill said, *but it seems like a weirdly invasive thing to just ask.*

The bear sighed dramatically and said, *Humans,* again in a tone that suggested it would never really understand Bill's reluctance to bring certain topics up.

Gwen finally pushed away from the stage, shaking herself. Her hair shivered in delightful waves, and her leather coat fell into place. Bill took a moment to be grateful that October in Colorado wasn't, mostly, all that cold yet, so she could get away with wearing a waist-length leather jacket instead of something sensible and warm that would cover her from the top of her head to her knees. It looked so *good* on her.

A hungry, horny little part of his brain informed him that it bet the coat would look even better *off* her, especially if all the rest of her clothes also mysteriously disappeared.

Bill said, "No," firmly and aloud, as if both his bear and his betraying brain would listen better that way. Gwen, coming back over to him, lifted her eyebrows curiously.

"No?"

"I was, uh." Bill scrambled for an explanation and landed on one that seemed plausible. "Telling myself not to look at the family chat, that's all."

"Brave of you." Gwen smiled up at him. "Is that a lion we need to beard in its den?"

"Bear," Bill said absently.

"...bear the lion in its den?" Gwen's eyebrows went

higher. "You know, I don't even know what that phrase means, exactly. Or I know what it *means*, obviously, but why beard?" She took her phone out, looking it up, and made a cheerful sound. "Oh! Kind of a combination of, like, grabbing you by the scruff to make you face the music," which she actually did, lifting her hand to curl it in the coarse hairs of Bill's short beard. He swallowed and covered her hand with his, making her notice what she'd done, and she was suddenly gazing up at him with those pale eyes swallowed by the darkness of her pupils. She wet her lips, and he had the incredible urge to bend and kiss her.

Before he could, Gwen said, "I'm so sorry," faintly, and tried to uncurl her fingers. He let her go immediately, his heart hammering at the missed opportunity, and she ducked her head, color staining her cheeks before she glanced back up again. "I really am *so* sorry," she mumbled again. "I'm a pretty touchy-feely person but not usually with people I don't know well. I've had my hands all over you all day and it's really rude. I'm *very* sorry and I'll try not to do it anymore."

"It's okay," Bill said in a rush over the last words of her apology. "I really don't mind. I'm not used to it. I'm big and people usually try to avoid me. But I don't mind."

"Still." Her smile was embarrassed. "Still, I'll try not to be so weird. Anyway, it's partly 'beard' because grabbing you—grabbing *someone*—by the beard is a way to draw their attention, and partly because I guess people maybe used to use 'beard' to mean 'face' so it's kind of a pun, face the lion in its den. I never heard 'bear the lion in its den' before, though. Oh, you probably meant beard the bear in its den." She laughed, letting her embarrassment drain away. "I'm not sure about that, though. Bearding the bear in his den sort of sounds like being the fake girlfriend for the big gay guy when he goes home." Her eyes suddenly went round. "Oh. Do you need that kind of beard?"

"No!" Bill's voice rose so fast it nearly broke on the single, short syllable. "No, no! God, of all the various problems with my family, that's not one of them. I'm straight, but they wouldn't care if I brought home a boyfriend. I mean, they'd be really confused, because I'm straight, but…"

Maybe, his bear suggested, *you should stop talking now.*

That, Bill thought, was a *very* good idea.

Gwen was grinning up at him, all her own embarrassment clearly forgotten. "Good."

"Which part?"

Her grin got wider. "All of it. Especially that you're straight, though." As Bill's heart soared, she added, "Look, I gotta go back to the pub to get my guitar, if nothing else. If you *do* need to talk to your family and need backup, I'm happy to help."

"I just want them to know it's all under control."

Gwen reached for his hand, then, clearly remembering her promise to stop touching him so much, pulled hers back again, much to Bill's disappointment. "And it is. C'mon, big man. Let's go prove it to them."

CHAPTER 9

Gwen hadn't really thought Bill was gay, although there'd been a moment there where she'd been shocked at the crushing dismay she'd felt at the idea he might be. He had kind of a weird thing about bears—the comment about bearding a bear in his den had been the second one he'd made about them in the few hours she'd known him—but *fond of wildlife* didn't even rank in the list of strange things her exes had been into. Maybe there was a bear rescue or sanctuary near Renaissance. That would make sense, with it being at the foot of the Colorado mountains, and Bill seemed like the kind of guy who might volunteer somewhere like that.

He kept saying thank you as they drove back to the pub, until Gwen had to put her hands up, palm out, like she was creating a physical wall. "Look, you don't have to thank me. I want this weekend to go well, too. It doesn't do either of us any good if it's a bust, so if it helps, you can think of me doing this gig at the

Harlequin as covering my own ass, okay? Trust me, I've played for audiences who didn't want me there before, and it's no fun."

"Okay. It's just…" Bill shook his head, then nodded, and more firmly, said, "Okay. No more apologizing. Sorry."

There was a pause, and, at the stoplight, Bill briefly put his forehead against the steering wheel. Gwen started laughing, and when Bill lifted his head, he said, wryly, "I guess I'm bad at stopping apologizing. S—"

Gwen hooted laughter again as Bill clamped his mouth shut on another apology. She was still grinning as they pulled into the pub's parking lot, finding a space marked *staff* to park in. "You said your parents were driving up from Arizona? That's a long drive."

"Twelve hours or so, but Mom doesn't like flying. They got an EV as soon as they came on the market and they've driven pretty much everywhere since. I just have to…" Bill killed the engine and sat there a moment, staring at the pub's log-cabin walls. "I haven't really told them that things aren't going so well. They entrusted the business to me, and I'm just running it into the ground."

"Are you really?" Gwen asked quietly. "Is it that bad, or is it just not as good as it used to be?"

He wobbled a hand, still gazing at the building. "The brewery is doing really well. My younger brother Steve, the one who moved out to New York a few years ago, he's actually helped us expand across the upstate area there. People've really gone for our IPAs. And we reached market saturation in Colorado a while back so we've been expanding into the Pacific Northwest and starting to reach toward the east, too, and—" He broke off abruptly. "I'm good at that. I like that. The pub...I'm not good at running it. I thought I would be. How different could it be?"

Gwen laughed, hoping it didn't sound mean. "How different could running a pub be from running a brewery? I think they sound like *completely* different skills, Bill."

He gave her a startled look, blinked, and managed to look more surprised than he had before the blink. "I...I guess I hadn't thought of it that way? It's all our beer, after all."

"And your other brothers? The one I met, Laurie, and...Jon, did you say his name was? What are they good at?"

"They run the pub at the Faire every year. Not just here in Renaissance, but all over. It's part of how we've expanded into other states. They're great at it, but they want to do it at Faire, not here, stuck in one place day in and day out."

Gwen pursed her lips. "Well, something's going to have to change, isn't it? Either they have to step up or you have to find somebody else to run the pub so you can do the thing you're good at."

"But that's just it, that's where I'm failing my folks." Bill gave his head a big hard shake. "Look, though, you don't need to get caught up in all of this. I'm going to drag you down, and you've got shows to do all weekend."

"I have this strange desire to be caught up in all of

it," Gwen admitted with a smile. "I don't have much family, so maybe I find it all weirdly compelling." Or maybe she found Bill Torben compelling, although not at all weirdly. The big man with his dramatic pompadour hair just *delighted* her, and she wanted him to be happy even if she'd only known him a few hours. "Think your parents will be here before I have to be back at the Harlequin?"

"Maybe." Bill eyed her. "God, you're not proposing to meet my parents already, are you?"

Gwen laughed. "I guess I am. Don't worry, I'll try not to embarrass you."

"I don't think you could," Bill said. "You handled my brother just fine."

"He thinks a lot of himself," Gwen said absently, and a little too truthfully. Bill gave a sharp, startled laugh, and she winced. "I probably shouldn't have said that."

"Maybe, but you're not wrong. I'd think a lot of myself if I was that good-looking, too, though."

"Oh, believe me, next to you he's left wanting." Gwen swung out of the big truck without giving Bill a chance to respond, partly because she was afraid he wouldn't believe her, and partly because she was afraid she might lean over and hug him, or possibly kiss him, if she didn't. She'd thought he'd been going to kiss her back at the club, and her heart jumped again at the memory of his dark eyes gazing down into hers, and the warmth of his huge hands on her waist. She'd felt so very secure in that moment, as if nothing in the world could ever harm her.

Whatever Bill thought about her compliment, he'd

hidden it as he joined her at the front of the truck and they went into the building. She thought his gaze lingered on her a little longer than it might have otherwise, but it might have been her imagination.

What was *not* her imagination was that it was well after 5pm now, and the pub was considerably less busy than she would have expected it to be. The decor was still as clean and welcoming as before, but the only action in the place seemed to be at the bar itself, where Laurie Torben, who had pulled his hair back in a ponytail, was leaning on the counter flirting with a couple of women who seemed to appreciate it. Overall, it wasn't any busier than it had been at mid-afternoon, and Gwen suddenly understood Bill's concern. "Is it like this most nights?"

"Busier on the weekends, but yeah. It's like the light has gone out of the place." He sighed. "I guess my folks *were* the light."

"So we change the bulbs." Gwen smiled up at him, then startled as Laurie raised a hand and called out to Bill in a voice about an octave deeper than it had been that afternoon. "Dude, did he swallow a bullfrog since we saw him?"

"Oh." Bill grinned. "That's Jon, not Laurie. You haven't met him yet."

"No, I def..." Gwen trailed off, staring at the guy behind the counter. Now that he'd straightened up, she could see he was *maybe* shorter than the man she'd met that afternoon, and that his dark blonde hair was probably light brown, and wavier than Laurie's. His cheekbones were a little broader, and his jaw maybe a bit squarer, but he looked an *awful* lot like the guy she'd already met. "Are they twins?"

"They are not," Bill said with amusement. "Jon's older by eighteen months. All four of us definitely look like brothers, but Mom says she just used the same mold for those two because it was too much work to come up with a new one after three boys already. They're a huge hit at the Faires."

"I've gotta see a picture of all four of you," Gwen said incredulously. "That's crazypants."

"You should see our dad, too." Bill took out his phone. "Here, I've got a picture from Steve's wedding earlier this year. That's all of us. Steve's the one right next to me."

Gwen actually took the phone, squinted at the picture, laughed, and studied it again. Bill was right: the brothers *were* all cut from the same mold. He had the fanciest hair, with the terrific pompadour, and when the picture had been taken he'd been wearing a slightly longer, but well-trimmed, beard than he currently had. His brother Steve was both shorter and narrower than Bill, although not by much, and his own dark blonde hair was worn in a more conservative, but basically standard male haircut. The other two younger men in the photo still could have been twins, as far as Gwen was concerned, and all four of them sort of reminded her of the Hemsworth brothers: there was absolutely *no* doubt they were related, even if she thought Bill was easily the most attractive of the four.

But their dad was in the picture, too, and looking at him made Gwen laugh again. "You all look exactly like your father. I know what you'll look like in twenty years. The amazing thing," she said, still studying the picture, "is you all also look like your mom."

"Mom says she introduced the variations on the Torben theme," Bill said wryly. "I've got her eyes, Jon's got her cheekbones. Steve's jaw is a little slimmer, like hers. Laurie's got her mouth."

"The poor woman," Gwen said, handing the phone back. "She has no facial features left to herself."

"Well, she's got her nose left. We try to be polite about it. You know that old song 'Eyes Without A Face?' That's Mom, except she's 'Nose Without A Face.'"

Gwen laughed. "I'm really, *really* glad that's not true. She's really pretty, actually. Your whole family is. Crazypants lookalikes, but very good-looking."

"Tell Mom," Bill said with a smile. "She likes to take credit for making us."

"I will!" They'd been standing there talking long enough, ignoring Jon's greeting, that he was now staring at them curiously from behind the bar. "I think your brother is feeling neglected."

Bill, not quite enough beneath his breath to go unheard, said, "My brother is feeling amazed I'm talking to a woman," then put a smile in place and tilted his head toward the bar. "So I guess I should introduce you."

"It *cannot* be unusual for you to have a woman fawning over you," Gwen said without entirely thinking about what that implied. Or didn't imply, even. She'd just straight-up said she was fawning over him. She put a hand over her face and wondered if there was a ditch she could fling herself into, instead of dealing with the embarrassment of being herself.

For a guy who *had* to have women throwing themselves at him, Bill looked awfully pleased, though. "I haven't dated a lot recently. Been busy with the pub. But I'm glad you think I seem dateable. My brothers stopped believing I could meet women about ten years ago, I think." By that time they were at the bar and he was adding, "Hey Jonny. This is Gwen Booker."

"The accidental talent," Jon Torben said as he offered his hand. Gwen's eyebrows rose and he grinned. His smile was more lopsided than Laurie's, although that was still the most obvious-to-Gwen difference between himself and his younger brother. "No, I didn't come up with that on my own independent of Laurie. He posted it in the family chat, which," Jon said, eyeing Bill, "you haven't answered in *hours*."

"And look at that," Bill said in a tone that suggested this was a surprise to him, "the world hasn't even ended."

"No, but Mom's having palpitations. She and Dad will be here in an hour or so. So what's going on? I looked you up," Jon said to Gwen, "and you seem great, but you're, well. Not a jazz musician."

"I'm really not," Gwen agreed. "I'm gonna—" She cut herself off, suddenly aware that she was about to announce to one of Bill's family that *she* thought he should up-end the pub's whole business plan and do something completely different. That was *not* something she had any business announcing, or even doing. "I'm gonna get a drink and let you guys talk it out," she mumbled, and tried not to wince. Talk about a bad recovery.

Although neither of the Torben men seemed to notice. Bill even smiled at her. "Drinks are on the house."

"Aren't you lucky I'm a cheap date who only wants a soda, then?" Gwen wiggled her fingers at them in farewell, although since Jon was behind the bar, he actually got her the ginger ale she wanted, and Bill added, "Don't go far. If you leave me here, I'm not going to be able to escape so I can show up at the Harlequin on my own in a couple hours."

"Right. I'll be over there." Gwen pointed at an empty booth, then swiveled on her heel and went the other way. "As soon as I get my guitar…"

CHAPTER 10

Gwen sauntered away, all black leather, blue jeans, and attitude, and Bill admired that she could have that much attitude while holding a glass of ginger ale. As soon as she was out of earshot, Jon said, "So wh—" and Bill turned to grab his brother's upper arm.

"She's my *mate*!"

Watching Jon's jaw drop was worth having messed up the music booking for the weekend. His eyes rounded and he cranked his head around to watch Gwen disappear into the back hall, then returned to gaping at Bill. "*She*? Is *your* mate? Oh my God! Why didn't you tell the family chat?" His voice rose until he squeaked.

Bill nearly clapped his hand over Jon's mouth. "Shh! She doesn't know yet, obviously! And I've been with her every minute since we met, so I haven't had time to tell anybody! And yes! *She* is *my* mate! You don't have to sound so surprised!"

"Well, dude, I mean, like..." Jon apparently didn't have much more of an argument than that, although he rallied after a minute. "She's just kind of edgy for a guy like you, isn't she? You're kind of a stay-at-home business owner type, and she's..." His gaze went after her again, although Gwen was nowhere in sight. "A rock star?"

"Maybe I need a little edgy in my life," Bill muttered. "I know she's my mate, Jon. I *felt* it."

"So you didn't screw up."

"What?"

Jon shrugged, shaking Bill's hand off his arm. "If she's your mate, then there's no way you screwed up the booking, that's all I'm saying. You might not have booked the person you meant to, but you definitely didn't book the *wrong* person. Not if fate was involved."

Bill felt his own jaw drop as his bear, placidly, said, *See? Nothing's wrong.* Aloud, he managed to say, "Uh," and his brother gave him the crooked smile he was well-known for.

"Congratulations, man. I'm happy for you. When are you going to tell her?"

"Oh, God." Bill sat on a bar stool and dragged his hands down his face. "I have no idea. I have no idea how to. And I don't want to add that on top of trying to find a crowd for a rock band instead of a jazz quartet. I haven't looked at the numbers," he added grimly into his palms. "How many tickets have been canceled?"

"About twenty percent so far. The free beer to offset the disappointment was a good promotional idea."

"It was Gwen's," Bill said, still into his hands, and Jon laughed.

"Really? She's sharp as well as hot, then, huh? That's great. Honestly, bro." He socked Bill's shoulder lightly, then did it again until Bill looked up at him. "Tell Mom and Dad. They'll unclench."

"I don't know. There's a lot of other stuff I need to catch them up on."

"Well, then, let me make a sage suggestion: catch them up on all of it, *then* tell them you found your mate. It'll make them forget anything else short of the pub actually burning down." Jon made a show of looking around. "Which it's not doing. So it'll all be good, bro. Don't worry so much. You always did worry too much."

"Somebody's got to."

"Do they?" Jon punched his shoulder again and got him a beer that Bill gazed into longingly.

"Gwen's doing a drop-in gig at the Harlequin tonight. I'm supposed to go over with her, so I shouldn't drink."

"Let her drive," Jon suggested. "She just got a ginger ale, so she's obviously not drinking herself, and then you'll be stuck with one car all night. Like only one bed, except with wheels."

"Jon..." Bill lifted the beer, which was one of their most popular, the Thunder Blunder Crystal Malt, and stared through the golden bubbles at his brother's glass-distorted figure. "The 'only one bed' thing is a forced proximity for sexy times trope, and I am *not* hooking up with Gwen in a car. I was too tall for that by the time I was seventeen, and I'm bigger all over than I was then."

Jon held up his hands. "I do *not* need to hear how big you are, all over or anywhere else."

"Oh my God, Jon! You're thirty years old! You don't have to be this juvenile!" Bill put the beer down to glare at his brother. The beer slopped over his hand, and he muttered, first licking it off because he was a man of great dignity, then, grumpily, drying his hand, the glass, and the counter with a napkin before draining most of the beer in one go. It really *was* a good beer, he thought irritably, then shook his head, not even sure why he'd gotten grumpy. Because everything was all too much, he guessed.

Everything is too much, his bear agreed. *Don't do everything. Just be with our mate.*

I wish it was that easy, Bill said.

Why isn't it?

He sighed. *Because it just isn't, when you're human.*

The bear sent an image of them bumbling happily through the woods in bear form, raiding honey or eating berries before napping in a den they'd dug in some tree roots. Then, thoughtfully, it added the idea of Gwen napping with them, all cuddled up snuggly warm against the bear's belly.

Bill couldn't help chuckling. *I'm going to have to explain the whole shifter thing before we can do that, buddy. For all I know she'll scream and run off into the woods on her own.*

Then we'll chase her! the bear suggested happily, then paused. *As long as she doesn't run very far.*

As long as she doesn't run far, Bill agreed, amused. It was probably better to let the bear imagine a human could out-pace it on a distance run, although the truth was, even true bears could move a lot faster than humans over at least a couple of miles. Shifter bears had considerably more stamina and a far greater ability to judge their pacing, so in the hypothetical situation where they were chasing Gwen through the woods, she was in trouble.

His bear gasped. *Our mate is not in trouble from us!*

Another chuckle escaped Bill's chest, and he had the impulse to give his bear a hug.

Bear hugs, it said with satisfaction.

Bear hugs, Bill agreed, and Jon, watching him, said, "That's better. Your bear's reassuring you, isn't it?"

"Something like that." Bill passed a hand over his eyes and glanced at his younger brother. "How are you doing?"

"Oh, you know, keeping busy. I'm actually glad the Faire season is over this year. I don't think I've slept since May."

"I guess it's just about time to hunker down and hibernate, then."

Jon squinted thoughtfully at some distant thing. "Have you ever wanted to try? Just...forget about humaning, go see if you can sleep from December through March?"

"You have no idea," Bill said, heart-felt, and Jon pulled his gaze from the distance to smile at him.

"But who'd get things ready for Faire then, right?

We miss you at it, you know that? Steve was never as into it, but you used to be good."

"Somebody's got to run this place, Jon."

"Yeah, I guess there's that. Your girl's back," he added with a lift his his chin toward one of the booths. Bill turned to see Gwen sprawled in it, her guitar across the table and her phone in her hands as she typed lightning fast with her thumbs. "You should go tell her."

"I've only known her for four hours!"

"No time like the present, right? No?" Jon smiled again at Bill's desperate glare. "All right, no. Are you gonna hang out long enough to see Mom and Dad when they get here, or would you rather not introduce her to the parents four hours after she met you?"

"Believe it or not, *she* suggested she meet them about *three* hours after I met her."

"It's fate, bro!" Jon clapped a hand to his heart theatrically, then laughed. "Oh. I guess it really is."

"I don't think I've ever met anybody as *confident* as she is," Bill said a little dazedly. "She blew in here like a rock star—" He broke off with a rough laugh, but turned his hands up, indicating it was true metaphorically as well as literally. "—turned my life upside down, found out what I'd done wrong, and just threw herself into fixing it as best she could all within about five minutes. It's like she never met anything she didn't think she could handle."

"Well, in that case Mom and Dad will be a breeze," Jon said. "First because they're really pretty easy-going, and second because you know Mom's been dying for us all to meet our mates and settle down and have a series of large, bear shifter babies, so she'll be thrilled, and if she's happy, Dad's happy."

"Right. Because what rock stars want is to stop their careers to have babies."

"Didn't slow Mick Jagger down any, did it?"

Bill stared at his brother. "Mick Jagger had the easy part, you idiot."

Jon turtled his chin in, looking startled. "Well, I guess that's true. I hadn't thought of that."

"You're an actual Neanderthal. Except I think that's probably doing an injustice to Neanderthals. Seriously, how did the same parents raise us? You *know* how hard Mom worked with four kids."

Jon said, "I guess," in a tone that suggested he hadn't thought much about that, either.

For the first time, it dawned on Bill that as the oldest, he probably had a much clearer idea of just how hard their mother *had* worked with four kids than any of his brothers, but especially Jon and Laurie. Jon had still been a toddler when Laurie was born. He wouldn't remember their mother's frazzled days or the hours of screaming babies and changing diapers the way Bill himself did. He said, "Jesus," under his breath, and then, aloud, added, "You need to go volunteer at a day care or something and get an idea of how much work kids are, man."

"I think you have to be *vetted* to work at a day care, bro. And probably trained in childcare or something. I don't think they let randos walk in off the street."

"You know what I mean, Jon. Anyway, yeah, if Mom and Dad get here before we have to leave for

Gwen's pick-up gig, I'm introducing her. But not as my mate." He gave Jon a gimlet eye. "And you're not either. Not until I've got a chance to explain it all *to* her."

Jon raised his hands in surrender. "I wouldn't dare."

That, at least, Bill thought was probably true. He nodded, finished the rest of his beer, and with a wave, left Jon at the bar so he could join Gwen at her booth. Although really, he stopped at the edge of her booth, aware she was involved in her texting. "Mind if I join you?"

She glanced up from her phone with a smile, and he was shocked all over again by the pale electric blue of her eyes. "Please do. I'm posting to the Fits groups."

Bill slid into the other side of the booth, laughing. "'The Fits.' Is it weird calling them that?"

Gwen wrinkled her nose, which was an incredibly cute gesture completely at odds with her winged eyeliner and red slash lipstick. "So weird, but they named themselves, so who am I to argue? And it's better than calling them our 'followers.' Then it sounds like I'm a cult leader."

"I think rock stars kind of are."

"No, they're cult *figures*," Gwen disagreed like she'd thought about it. "It'd be much worse if they were cult leaders. Generally you don't want somebody with legions of fans telling people what to do. Anyway, the chat rooms are afire and there are a bunch of people planning road trips, and it turns out I've got some hardcore enthusiasts right here in River City."

"…this is…Renaissance?"

Gwen laughed out loud. "Oh, no. Not a musical fan?"

"I'm not...*not* a musical fan. I just don't know much about them...?"

"Oh, we're going to have to fix that."

Bill's heart lurched. On one hand, Gwen Booker was his mate, and he knew that meant that one way or another, they would be together. On the other, the very idea that she was planning—no matter how frivolously—to make sure he saw some musicals suggested she *wanted* to spend more time with him, and somehow that seemed more concrete than something as whimsical as fate. He suddenly felt like he needed something to do with his hands, and wished he'd brought the beer glass to the table even if it was empty.

Gwen, blissfully unaware of his emotional turmoil, smiled at him. "It's a line from a song in *Music Man.* Or part of a line. Point is, I've got some fans coming to the Harlequin tonight and are showing off the receipts for the tickets tomorrow and Saturday. See, it's all going to work out."

For the first time in a long time, Bill thought he might actually believe that.

CHAPTER 11

*B*y the time Gwen finished her ginger ale, a surprising number of people had chimed in on her social media fronts to proclaim their intention of showing up at the brewpub by 8pm the next evening. "Look at this," she said in delight, and got up to sit next to Bill so he could read her phone screen with her. He scooted over in the booth, leaving most of a warm spot for her to sit in. His scent was absolutely delicious, kind of outdoors musky mixed with a malty smell that she figured must be from the beer-making. It was distracting, and even though she had her phone *right there,* for a moment she couldn't remember what she'd wanted to show him.

"All those people are coming?" Bill asked in surprise.

That cleared Gwen's head—kind of—and she nodded enthusiastically. "I figured we'd get some from Denver and Colorado Springs and everything, but I wasn't counting on anybody from out of state. But there are people coming from California! Chicago!

Look at GemJones9921! She's *driving* from *Seattle!* Obviously she won't be here until the Saturday night gig."

"Obviously," Bill echoed, sounding bemused. "You're kind of famous, aren't you? Mike mentioned it, but I didn't realize quite who I'd booked."

"Mmph." Gwen rolled her shoulders uncomfortably. "I'm not can't-walk-down-the-street famous, but I have fans, yeah. I told you they'd rally."

"I know, but I didn't think it was a 'drive from Seattle' kind of rallying. That's pretty cool, Gwen. Can I ask you something?"

"As long as it's not something like 'what kind of diet are you on that you stay in such good shape' or 'how are you going to manage being a rock star and having children', yeah."

Bill blinked, clearly taken aback. "Do people ask you things like that?"

"You wouldn't *believe* some of the stuff I've been asked."

"Hnh." The single sound seemed offended on her behalf. "Well, if you ever need somebody swatted for that kind of question, I volunteer."

Gwen laughed and balled up her fist. "Thanks. I've got a mean right hook, but playing guitar with a broken hand is hard."

"I'm at your service," the big man promised. "Anyway, I wanted to ask what happened with your fir—oh, God, they brought the cousins." A commotion at the door interrupted him, and Gwen, who couldn't see over the tops of the booths like he could, leaned side-ways to find out what was going on.

A whole *passel* of people were trying to get through the door together. Gwen didn't normally think in terms of 'passels,' but in this particular case, they really struck her as a passel. There were eight or nine of them, two of whom she recognized from Bill's family photo: his parents were in the midst of the passel. Both of them were taller than she expected, although his dad wasn't as tall as any of the brothers she'd met so far. His mom was almost dwarfed by the people around her, although she had to be at least five ten herself. It was just that everybody else was enormous. There were two women, both easily over six feet, and the rest were men, all of them taller than Bill's father, who matched one of the women in height.

Gwen clapped a hand over her mouth and completely failed to muffle a laugh. Bill groaned and put his head on the table momentarily. "I know. We all look alike."

"You *really do*," Gwen squeaked through her fingers. The passel all bore a *strong* family resemblance to Bill himself, although they had more variation in hair color than the Torben brothers did. Every single one of them was attractive, in a cookie-cutter way. "Is there an actual assembly line?"

"My aunts and mother would tell you no," Bill said, still with his head on the table. "But you should have seen the whole gang at Steve's wedding this summer. At least my cousin who met his faa—uh, his girlfriend there had the decency to fall for a tiny blonde. The men in my family tend to go for statuesque amazons, leading to giant children."

A startling sense of crushing disappointment took Gwen's breath away for a moment. She wasn't short by any means. In fact, she was often surprised at how tiny other women were. But she also didn't come anywhere near *statuesque.*

It amazed her how much she wanted to be amazonian enough to catch Bill Torben's attention.

"Tell you what." Bill had lifted his head, although he'd also slid down into the booth as far as he could go, like he was trying not to be noticed. "In about ten seconds here, my idiot brother is going to tell that group of lunatics that I'm over here, but you have time to escape. You wanted to meet my *parents*, not my entire clan. What are they all doing here!" It wasn't a question, just an exclamation of despair, and Gwen, despite her promise to keep her hands off him, patted his arm reassuringly.

"They're probably here to rescue the weekend." The noise level in the pub had gone up about ten decibels with his family's arrival, and they seem to have quadrupled the number of people in the pub, just through their sheer size. "If I sneak out, are you going to be able to escape and get to the Harlequin?"

Bill, in the grim tone of a man who knew better, said, "Probably."

Gwen made an executive decision and grabbed his hand. "Get my guitar. Let's make a break for it."

"What? No, they'll see me—"

"There is *definitely* a door over there that leads out to the beer garden," Gwen said firmly. "We'll take it."

"They'll still see me! I'm six and a half feet tall!"

Gwen dipped a hand into her pocket and came out with a pair of earbuds. "Put these in. They're noise-canceling. You didn't hear them, that's all."

"They're *tiny*." Bill fumbled them into his ears, although they practically swam in his ear canals, because Gwen did, in fact, have fairly small ears, and used the smallest silicon tips that came with the buds. She was pretty sure Bill would have to buy XXL ones separately for his own purposes, then took a moment to wonder what other things he might have to buy in XXL.

That was *not* important right now.

"As long as the buds don't fall out between here and the beer garden door, that's enough excuse to not hear them," she promised, then, her hand still wrapped firmly around Bill's, pulled the big man out of the booth and strode purposefully toward the back door. He grabbed her guitar case and followed, and to her relief, delight and amusement, nobody yelled *Bill!* until the door was almost closed behind them. She said, "Close enough!" and broke into a run. Bill yelped, trying to keep up while not letting the ear buds fall out, and clocked himself in the head with the guitar case. Gwen blurted, "Oh, God, sorry," and took the guitar so he could clap his hands over his ears and hurry along behind her.

"They're going to kill me," he announced a little too loudly.

Gwen flashed a grin over her shoulder at him. "First, not if they can't catch you, and second, nah, you're bigger than all of them, and I bet I'm meaner. She-bear, rawr." She made claws with her hands, swiping, and although she laughed, she swore that Bill Torben actually did heart eyes at her. It was about the cutest thing she'd ever seen, even if 'cute' and 'giant man' didn't usually go together in her expectations. "Come on, into my getaway car." She opened the Chevy's back door and tucked the guitar in with more care than she took slinging herself into the front seat a moment later, and Bill climbed in, suddenly looking particularly enormous in the comparatively small space. "Sorry I can't slide the seat back. My feet won't reach the pedals if I do. That's the problem with bench seats."

"There are worse fates." Bill stretched his legs out as best he could as she pulled out of the parking lot. "I can always ride with the guitar in the back if I have to."

"Ah, yes," Gwen said in her best British accent. "I'm Lord William Torben and I wish to not be disturbed as I'm ferried home, James."

Bill laughed. "Yeah, but if I was upper-class British and my last name was pronounced 'Torben' it would probably look like it was pronounced 'Troughburn' or something."

"Troughstiltenburn," Gwen suggested. "The 'stilten' is silent."

He laughed again. "Yeah. Like that. Or maybe with a 'shire' in there somewhere. Do you actually know where you're going?"

"Yes." After a beat, Gwen added, "I do not, however, know how to get there, so if you could navigate…?"

"Hah! Yeah, turn left up there."

It was a shorter drive to the Harlequin than Gwen expected, probably because they'd gone there via the ice cream and coffee cafe earlier, and she hadn't been paying much attention on the way back. They arrived much earlier than they needed to, and Mike Piccolo met them almost before they came in the door. "Saw you pulling up on the security cameras. You have quite a few fans here already, Gwen. You want me to take you around to the stage entrance?"

"Nah, I can't help set up if I'm hiding backstage. Besides, I've got a giant personal bodyguard if anything gets hairy, which I don't think it will." She knocked her shoulder against Bill's arm. "If that's okay with you?"

"I'll guard your body any time," he promised.

Gwen laughed, and Piccolo looked between them with amusement. "If you say so. Want me to take your guitar backstage, at least?"

"That, yes, please, seems like a good idea. I'm not fragile, but expensive musical instruments can be." As she handed her guitar over, Gwen heard somebody say, "Oh my God, it really *is* her," and then suddenly half a dozen people were ringing her, their expressions full of nervous delight.

She raised her hands and said, "Nope!" firmly, then pointed over their heads at a table near the stage. "You can go there. I'll come to you, but I'm not going to be a fire hazard and block the front doors, all right?"

A shy titter rushed through the little group and at

least two of them mumbled apologies as they all scurried toward the table she'd pointed at. Gwen took a breath, squaring her shoulders, and glanced up to see Bill gazing down at her with awe in his dark eyes. "You don't need a bodyguard, do you?"

"Welllllll...." Gwen laughed and shook her head. "Not with half a dozen kids barely old enough to be in the club, no. Not with most fans, really. They're usually eager but well-meaning. It's when they get too freaked out to remember I'm a person too, that it gets to be a problem. But I tell you what, having six and a half feet of backup does not *hurt* when you tell people to go over there and wait for you. C'mon, they're settled down now, so we can go over." She did, joining her fans at a table and swinging a chair around to sit on it backward, and beamed at their excited faces. "Thank you for being here. This is a totally off-the-cuff thing before the gigs at the Thunder Bear Brewpub this weekend and I wasn't sure if anybody was going to show up!"

A wall of protestations met her self-deprecation, and for the next half hour or so she chatted, signed things, took selfies, and was very aware of Bill Torben's big, reassuring presence at her back as more people came in, realized she was there, and came to have a moment with her themselves. Eventually she clapped her hands together and rose, smiling at everybody. "Look, I promised I'd help set up so the house band didn't think I was a total bitch, so I'm gonna go get started with that. It was amazing to meet all of you!"

Voices chorused excited goodbyes, and Gwen felt

the warmth of Bill's hand at the small of her back as he ushered her away, murmuring, "You're really good at that."

"I've been doing it half my life," she replied. "It's not hard, but it's nice to have somebody at my back. You make me feel really safe."

By then they were at the stage, and Bill took a moment to look down at her before she left him. "It's all I want," he said. "I want you to be safe and happy."

Gwen's heart fluttered and she ducked her head, blushing, before she looked back up at him with a smile. "Well, you've got the pub to think of, too, so maybe it's not *all* you want, but thanks, big man. That makes me feel good." She vaulted up on stage before she risked something silly like kissing him, and dared a look over her shoulder as she strode toward the wings.

Bill Torben was watching her like she really *was* all he wanted in the world. Gwen's heart fluttered again, and instead of scolding herself, she decided to use that feeling as she went to play the role of rock star.

CHAPTER 12

$\mathcal{B}$ ill had really wanted to pick Gwen up and put her on the stage, like he'd taken her down earlier. He barely stopped himself, mostly because he was aware of her fans—her *fans*, because she was a *rock star* who lived in a whole different stratosphere than he did—were watching, and he didn't know how fast they would spread gossip on the internet. He was, however, sure that they would, if they watched their idol being lifted onto the stage by a guy who was supposed to be her bodyguard.

Bodyguards, though, didn't want to make sure their wards were safe and happy beyond anything else in the world. Safe, maybe, but not necessarily happy. And Bill had meant that. He'd throw the whole pub over if it meant keeping Gwen both safe and happy.

For now, however, he was pretty sure looming at the stage's edge wasn't helpful to her, so he backed off, trying to find somewhere that he could both see and wouldn't block everybody else's line of sight. He eventually backed himself into a corner and stood hunched, as if there might be someone in the wall behind him, watching as the club began to fill.

There were a *lot* of people. If they could get a third of these numbers at the pub over the weekends, and even a fifth of them over the week, they'd be beating business off with a stick. Bill shook his head. He knew a club was a different kind of scene from a pub, but maybe Gwen was right, and they needed to try catering to a different crowd. The Thunder Bear had passed down to a new generation. Maybe it was time for the clientele to change, too.

"Hey. Bill." Mike Piccolo, his silver hair gleaming different colors in the club's changing lights, appeared at Bill's side and tilted his head toward the stage. "Come on, I've got you VIP seating up at the front."

"Oh, no, I'm too big. People can't see over me. Thanks, though."

The older man smiled, although there was a surprisingly steely look in his eyes. "Maybe people can't see over you, but Gwen can't see *you* if you're lurking back here in the corner."

"I don't think that's a problem?"

"Young man," Mike said with the authority of someone who was his parents' friend, "that girl is here to try to help *your* pub do well this weekend. It's obviously good for her if the gigs go well, but the talent doesn't go to this kind of trouble for anybody unless they really want to. She invited you to see her perform tonight, didn't she?"

Bill, feeling inexplicably guilty, nodded, and Mike's

gaze got steelier. "So make sure she can see *you* seeing her perform, and get your big ass down to the VIP seating."

"My ass," Bill said in an attempt at injured dignity, "isn't proportionately big." But he went, slinking toward the VIP booth that turned out to have a *Reserved* sign on it, and his name scrawled on a piece of paper on the table. It turned out Mike had thought about where to put him, though, because the booth, while elevated, was also off to one side and had rela- tively little space behind it, so there wouldn't be all that many people crowding around and trying to see past him. Somehow that genuinely made him feel better, and he found himself suddenly looking forward to the performance in a way he hadn't been just a minute or two earlier.

Which was ridiculous, since he wasn't any less eager to see Gwen sing. But he slowly realized that hiding in the back hadn't made him feel like he was *part* of the evening, and this VIP seat, where he could see clearly— and where Gwen would be able to see him—made him feel like he belonged.

Bill wasn't actually sure when he had last really felt like he *belonged* somewhere. Maybe when he'd still been working the Renaissance Faires with his brothers. He knew it wasn't that he didn't belong, or in some way wasn't welcome at the pub. It was just...that was work. He was *necessary* there, but somehow that didn't feel quite the same as belonging there.

The stage lights suddenly went down, bringing an

unexpected—to Bill, at least—cheer from the crowd, which had filled up the club pretty comfortably already. People moved closer to the stage, anticipation flooding the air, and he couldn't help smiling. It had been years since he'd been at a gig anywhere other than the pub. To his surprise, he was already enjoying it.

There was movement on the stage, easily visible to his shifter-enhanced dark vision. Bears were particularly adept at picking out movement in the dark, too, so he was able to watch Gwen swagger on stage, absolutely certain of herself even in the darkness. The crowd could see, or sense her, as well, and another cheer went up before the lights burst back on and there was Gwen Booker, rock star, standing in the spotlight.

This time the roar made Bill laugh, and his bear sat up warily, wondering if that huge sound was another bear, or some other kind of threat. *It's just everybody appreciating Gwen,* Bill told it, and got a tremendous sense of satisfaction from the animal.

*Everyone **should** appreciate our mate.* It settled back down, trusting Bill's comfort, and he, in turn, leaned forward, drawn to Gwen's.

She yelled, "Hello, Renaissance!" and over the shouted greetings in response, added, "Hello, *Harlequin!*" That time the cheers drowned her out, or would have, if she'd been doing anything but grinning. God, she was beautiful, Bill thought. Not just beautiful. Magnetic. He couldn't imagine anyone being able to take their eyes off her, even if she was only standing there grinning at them all. "All right!" she called. "It's really early for a jam, and the house band and me, we've never played together before, so look, you all are just gonna have to put up with listening to our warmups, all right?"

Another roar met the question, and by that time, Bill was almost laughing with pleasure. The crowd was so happy to see her, and Gwen herself was obviously thrilled to be there. Someone yelled the name of a song as a request, and she sauntered down to the stage's lip to stare into the crowd as if they'd been rude. "Really? *Really?* Is that how you think it's gonna go? We're gonna come up here, never having played together before, and take *requests?*"

The same voice said, "Yes?" hopefully, and Gwen burst out laughing.

"All right, all right, let's see what we can do, but hey, don't get cocky, okay? What's your name? Rudy? Listen, Rudy, we got a real set list and everything, like we know what we're doing, and you can't be out there just pretending this whole thing is a private audience just for you." She walked back up the stage, dropping the mic she'd been carrying down to her hip, and leaned into say something in the guitarist Ripley's ear. They laughed and nodded, and she went to the other people on stage—a long-haired bassist, a keyboardist, and a drummer—speaking to them, too. Whatever she said made them laugh as well, and then with a nod she returned to center stage and the spotlight, pointing at the person who'd made the request. "Okay, just this once, Rudy, this one's for you."

Another cheer rose, then turned into club-wide laughter as the band, and Gwen, all started the requested song, but each in a different key or with the wrong beat, or—Bill didn't even know *what* else they were doing wrong, but it sounded genuinely awful. Gwen sang several phrases, her voice going all over the place, before breaking down into giggles against the mic. "Told you you shouldn't ask a new band to play that cold!"

The drummer, while she was laughing, called out a beat, and the second time they started the song right, getting another laughing roar of approval that set the tone for the rest of the evening. After the warmup, by the time the set was supposed to actually start, the club was full, and half an hour after that, it was packed. Gwen played to the crowd fabulously, occasionally taking requests after checking with the band to make sure they could follow, and once actually taking her phone out to apparently send them all the sheet music for a song they didn't know. That earned her a huge cheer that she bowed to the audience for, then bounced around the stage asking people their names and whether they were going to the Thunder Bear tomorrow while the band looked over the sheet music. A few minutes later they were playing again, raising the roof and encouraging dancers and singing along. It was a jubilant evening that left Bill's ears ringing when the band finally left the stage after an encore.

The audience shouted for another, and to Bill's surprise, Gwen came back on stage alone, guitar slung across her body and her mic in one hand. She brought it to her mouth, murmuring, voice low and warm and inviting as she said, "Here's the deal, folks. I've got a new album coming out next year, and some music nobody's ever heard. But you guys probably want the stuff you already kno—" She was drowned out by the cries of protest, and ended up laughing into the mic. "Really? You sure? You wanna close on weird new music? All right." She grinned at them all, that delicious dark wine lipstick making her smile sweet enough to cut through the whole night. "Tell you what. I'll do two songs tonight, and two each on the nights I'm playing over at the Thunder Bear this weekend. You come to all three gigs, you'll have heard almost half the songs on the new album. That sound good?"

She was barely audible over the cheers of approval and excitement, but the audience settled as she patted her palms downward, asking them to quiet a bit. And they were *rapt*, Bill thought, as she sang one of her new songs, as if every single one of them was holding their breath, listening with their whole beings. By the third chorus for both songs, people were joining in, already committing the melody and words to memory, and Gwen herself looked as if she could fly for joy. The second song blended into a third that got a roar of excitement as the first bars became clear to the crowd, who sang along lustily with this one. At the end, Gwen bowed, waved, and walked off stage to a howl of protest that went on for three or four minutes, until the audience was sure she wouldn't come out for another encore. The crowd started breaking up, people going to get drinks or moving farther away from the dance floor, and after a while, Mike Piccolo made his way up to Bill's booth and sat down with a grin. "Your girl knows how to play to a crowd."

"She was amazing," Bill said dazedly. He could still feel the music in his blood, and his ears were ringing in the aftermath of the performance. "I can't believe how many people showed up tonight."

"Free gig," Mike said, though his smile said he knew it was more than that. "You're going to be busy at the pub this weekend."

"Let me know if you want to come. I'll send over some tickets. This has been—thank you. This was great."

"Hey." Mike chuckled. "Don't imagine it was altruism. I sold a lot of alcohol tonight and didn't have to pay for the talent. And Ripley's over the moon."

"I think everyone is."

"Yeah, but not everybody got to get up on stage with their guitar hero." Mike grinned and stood, offering a hand to shake. "No way Gwen's coming through the front of the house again tonight. She'd never get out of here. I'll take you backstage."

Bill glanced at the crowd. "That'll draw attention, won't it? Is there already a mob at the stage door?"

"Not too bad."

"Then I'll go around and meet her there, maybe. Maybe we can get out early enough that most of them won't think she'll be ready to leave yet." Bill took his phone out to text Gwen, winced at the number of unread messages in the family chat, and sent a note saying, *Let me know when you're ready to go.*

Any time, came back immediately.

Meet you at the stage door in a minute, he wrote back, then nodded at Mike. "Thank you again."

"Send those tickets over," Mike said with a grin. "I want to be there the night Gwen Booker breaks big."

CHAPTER 13

The only thing better than performing was sex, and in the high after coming off stage, Gwen was never even sure about that. She had to look to make sure her feet were still on the ground, and after exchanging hugs with Ripley and the other members of the house band, she wasn't sure any of them were still earth-bound. "That was a great show," she said to all, and each of them. "Playing with you guys was an honor. Thank you so much."

The bassist, a long-haired guy in his sixties, gave her a laconic nod, and the drummer and keys player, both closer to her own age, grinned and bumped shoulders but weren't beside themselves about playing with her. That was fine: this was their job, and Gwen was just another lead singer. She knew that, and so did they.

So, technically, did Ripley, but they were still vibrating with joy and excitement, because—and Gwen knew *this*, too—this was the biggest gig they'd ever done. The biggest star they'd ever performed with.

It was funny, Gwen thought, that she could be run of the mill and star of the show all at the same time. That was what kept her balanced, she figured. The people who were overwhelmed by getting to share a stage with her were evened out by the ones who thought it was just another day on the job. She grinned, hugged Ripley again, said, "See you tomorrow," and headed out, her heart leaping at the thought of Bill Torben waiting at the stage door for her. She'd had a lot of guys wait for her, over the years, and she could tell a lot about how the relationship would go from the first glimpse she had of them after a show.

Not that she was in a relationship with Bill. Or expecting to be in one. She was only in Renaissance for the weekend. Gwen almost literally kicked herself, reminding herself of that, but the reminder felt flat and disappointing. "Woo, girl," she said beneath her breath as she pushed the stage door open. "You got it bad!" There were worse things than a weekend crush, though.

Bill Torben, all six and a half feet of him, was right there at the stage door, putting a hand on it, well above Gwen's head, to control how far it opened, to give her a chance to gauge the crowd and, clearly, to make sure they couldn't surge forward and push her back inside the building, or up against the closing door if she stepped out too fast. He held it effortlessly, although she could see the muscles in his arm at play, and when she lifted her eyes to his face, it was to find a small, awed smile on the big man's face, and a softness in his eyes that she'd never seen in a man before. He breathed, "You were *incredible*," and then, just as quietly, added, "There are about twenty people out here. How do you want to play this?"

Oh, this was one *hell* of a weekend crush.

The rush of voices calling her name, squealing with excitement, cheering, all the sounds that she was used to at a stage door finally came in, as if Bill's very presence had blocked them out, giving her a little space just to be herself in. Gwen's heart contracted hard again and she gave him what felt like an unusually tentative smile. "I can sign things or do selfies, but only if they can line up and be polite. Do you think you can get them to do that?"

He winked, then, without releasing his incredibly strong grip on the door, turned his head to address the crowd in a startlingly deep, crisp, commanding voice. "Ms. Booker is prepared to sign albums and take selfies, *but only* if everyone calms down, lines up, and keeps their hands to themselves like decent, polite human beings. If you can't do that..."

Bill was a huge man anyway. He did something—took a breath, squared his shoulders, *something*—that made him look about three times his size, and his voice dropped another half octave. "If you can't do that, I'll be escorting Ms. Booker to her vehicle and *nobody* is going to bother her."

Beyond the stage door, someone audibly squeaked, and Gwen could see a quick shuffling of bodies as people rearranged themselves and quieted down. After a moment, Bill gave a firm nod and let the door open farther, revealing two tidy lines of wide-eyed fans, some clutching albums, some with their phones lifted, somebody with a Sharpie and their arm bared to be signed, all of them looking like nervous first-graders who had been promised ice cream after school if they could just be *quiet* while in line. At the very end of the line, a few people were still arranging themselves in what looked like a 'you-go-first, no-you-go-first, no-you-i-insist' kind of disagreement of who could be politest, but they got themselves sorted out as Gwen bit down on a giggle.

"Amazing," she announced to all of them. "This is incredible. I need you guys to come to every stage door and teach other people how to line up politely like this."

They *did* giggle, and for the next few minutes Gwen was busy signing, giving hugs, and getting selfies. Bill moved down the line with her, doing an incredible job of staying out of the way while also being an absolutely unmistakable Presence that no one wanted to risk messing with. A few more people came out of the club before she reached the end of the line, and she signed things for them, too, but grimaced faintly as a larger group came out, their voices incredibly loud and some-what inebriated-sounding as they echoed off the parking lot concrete. One of them shouted as they glimpsed Gwen, who braced herself, but Bill seemed attuned to every nuance of her body language and murmured, "Go ahead and go to your car, if you want. I'll be right behind you," before planting himself firmly between Gwen and the drunken group.

Gwen, glancing over her shoulder as she headed for the Chevy, saw a bunch of the oncoming crowd visibly deflate and give up after one look at Bill's large self blockading the easiest path to her. A few, more determined or more intoxicated, approached him, but as she got in the Chevy she noticed none of them went *past* him. It was like he was so big the idea of going around just didn't cross their minds. She grinned, turned the engine on, and waited the minute or two it took him to dissuade the smaller group. To her surprise, they didn't look at all pissy when he left them and came to get in the car with her. "What'd you say to them?"

Bill stretched his legs as best he could into the footwell. "That my fist was bigger than most of their faces and that they were welcome to try, if they wanted."

Gwen gave him a shocked look and he laughed. "No. I reminded them you'd be playing at the Thunder Bear all weekend and they had plenty of chances to meet you if they wanted to come to the other shows. I don't think I've physically threatened anybody since I was a linebacker in high school, and that was all action, not talk."

"Oh, so you're a man of action," Gwen purred, and to her delight, Bill Torben blushed again as she drove out of the parking lot. "You're a man of blushing, anyway."

"I've blushed more since I met you than in the past five years," Bill announced with a sense of outraged dignity. "It's you. You're affecting me."

"Is it okay if I like the sound of that?"

"Yeah." His voice softened enough to send a thrill through Gwen. "Yeah, it's great if you like the sound of that. You, ah. Mm. This has been an interesting day, with you. Better than I would have expected. And my God, Gwen. You were incredible up there on stage." His tone changed completely, from that low softness to pure pleased astonishment. "I can't believe you're not playing stadium tours."

An unexpected twist tightened Gwen's stomach, making nausea swim in her belly. She tried to swallow it down and fought for a smile. "Maybe some things aren't meant to be."

"I can't believe that."

"I can," Gwen said a little too sharply, and from the corner of her eye, caught Bill's concerned, interested glance. She braced herself for the inevitable questions, but to her surprise, after a few seconds, he only said, "You would know more about it than I do," and let it go, adding, "So what's the deal with the Impala? I was expecting a van."

"Ah." Gwen cleared her throat. "I had a crush on a tv character and when the Impala came up for sale I couldn't resist."

Bill laughed. "So the van life is a lie?"

"No, I do have one," she admitted. "I use it for longer tours, because living out of an Impala sucks. But this is just a weekend, and it's not a long drive, so I thought I'd live it up."

"Where are you from, anyway? Turn up there, the one way street gets us home faster than going back the way we came."

Gwen flicked the turn signal on. "I'm *from* Seattle, but I live in Denver."

"Really?" Bill gave her another startled look. "I didn't know you were that close."

"It's a good city to live in if you want to travel a lot of places. I do drive if I'm going on a tour, but if I've got a weekend gig, the airport can get me just about anywhere."

"So you're close enough we could—" Bill audibly broke off, then chuckled. "Drive out to see your gigs there. You play in clubs there, I assume?"

"At a few of them, yeah. I'll keep you posted if you want. Hey, I didn't say thanks for handling the fans back there at the Harlequin. If you ever need a new job as a door guy, I…totally can't pay you for that. Damn."

Bill laughed as they reached the Thunder Bear parking lot. "How could I refuse an offer like that? I'll be your door guy for the weekend, at least. I'm feeling optimistic," he admitted. "Total turnaround from when you blew in this afternoon. Oh, God, I didn't mean it like that."

"Are you sure?" Gwen parked the Impala and grinned at him. "Because you looked like your worst nightmare had just walked through the door."

"My face is a liar, then. I thought you were the most overwhelmingly cool person I'd ever seen." Bill puffed his cheeks out and gazed through the windshield at the pub. "But also, yes, kind of my worst nightmare, when I was expecting a little old white-haired lady with a jazz band. Oh, no. Did you get checked into the hotel? They were expecting Brooker, not Booker."

"I haven't even tried," Gwen said, surprised. "I came here first to check out the venue and then things went crazy."

Bill made a face. "Sorry. But at least I can call and let them know I had the name wrong. It's three rooms under your name? Well, Gwendolyn Brooker's name?"

"Yeah, my bassist and keys are a couple, and Penny says Sandy doesn't snore so she doesn't mind sharing with her."

"Implying you do snore?"

Gwen snickered. "Myles and Gemma say I don't, but when we've all crashed in the van a couple times on long trips Penny does sleep really badly, so either being on her own or sharing with somebody quiet is better for her. Not that any of that matters to you." Gwen smiled at him. "Tomorrow's going to be fine, Bill. The whole weekend is going to go well. Okay?"

"I'm starting to believe it." He took out his phone and called the hotel, correcting the name it was booked under, then hung up and nodded. "You're good to go. So we'll see you, what, tomorrow evening?"

"Oh, no. The band should show up around two and I'll be there to meet them, so that's the absolute latest I'll be there. You should expect me bright and early, though. I bet we can get some more promo done in the morning." She wrinkled her noise. "Okay, let me back-track that. 'Bright and early' has certain limitations when you're used to performing until midnight and staying up a few hours after that because you're on an adrenaline rush."

Bill made a show of looking at his phone to see the

time. "Well, it's only eleven thirty now, so you shouldn't be up past two, right? I'll expect you by eight a.m."

Gwen couldn't even *pretend* not to look horrified. Bill burst out laughing. "I was going to say six, but eight was obviously terrible enough. I'll see you when you get here, okay? This was a great evening, Gwen. Everything else aside, I haven't been out to a club like that in years, and I think it was really good for me. Thank you."

He hesitated, studying her, and Gwen's heartbeat quickened again. Before she could break the stalemate and lean in to kiss him, he ducked his head, said, "Good night," and left her to drive off to her hotel alone.

CHAPTER 14

There was valor and there was cowardice, and tonight, Bill decided he was a coward. First off, he was a coward for not kissing Gwen Booker. There'd been a look in her eyes that said she would have invited it, and he'd certainly wanted to, but somehow it seemed like he should try to explain the whole shifter thing *before* he started kissing her.

Mostly, though, he was a coward for sneaking to his truck and driving home instead of going into the pub to see how much of his family was left in there. For one thing, he knew for a fact that if he *did* go in, he would end up with at least two cousins staying at his three-bedroom ranch house a couple miles from the pub. It wasn't that he didn't want them to, exactly. It was more that it had been a hell of a day, and he wanted some quiet in which to sit down and contemplate it. All of it, but especially the fact that he'd met his fated mate, and that she was a rock star.

He really seemed like the least-likely person on

earth to be partner to someone like Gwen Booker. His bear, huffily, began a protest, and Bill shook it off as he got home and went inside. *I know,* he reassured the bear. *I believe it. It's just an idea that takes some getting used to, even for me. I don't know how I'm going to explain it to her.*

The bear settled, and Bill went to bed, convinced he'd be staring at the ceiling all night. Convinced he'd *better* be staring at the ceiling, and not stroking himself off thinking about Gwen. Even if the attraction was mutual—and he was fairly certain it was, mate bond aside—it seemed faintly rude somehow, like he should make his intentions to Gwen clear before he started getting off on active fantasies. The vague idea that it was rude didn't make keeping his hands folded firmly behind his head and not wrapped around his cock any easier, though eventually it did make him laugh at himself. He was pushing forty, not fourteen. A little discipline shouldn't require so much active contemplation.

Luckily—or not—sleep did claim him after a bit, and if his dreams were filled with rock stars, that was just fine with Bill.

AN INCESSANT BUZZING woke him not all that much later, although his phone—the source of the buzzing—claimed it was nearly nine in the morning, when he picked it up. Bill stared at the time a moment, trying to remember the last time he'd slept this late, then dropped the phone and collapsed back into bed. The incoming messages could wait a minute.

He couldn't remember the last time he'd ignored messages, either. Or the last time he'd woken up without a sense of grim doom hanging over him, for that matter. There was a strange lightness in his chest, like it was easier to breathe today than it had been in months, maybe years. He rubbed the heel of his hand against his sternum, half expecting some kind of mystical golden glow to arise, but instead a sensation of contentment settled into his bones in a way that was totally unfamiliar. For the first time since he'd taken over the pub, he felt like everything was going to be all right.

The phone buzzed again and this time he checked the messages, which was—of course—all from his family. Most of them were in the larger family chat, but a bunch were in the immediate family one, and the last of which, from Laurie, said, *The cinnamon rolls are gonna be gone before you get here, dude.*

Bill, blearily, said, "Cinnamon rolls?" and scrolled back in that chat, then switched to the other one, where an absolute wall of messages were moaning happily about cinnamon rolls, or bemoaning being too far away to have any. He scrolled up through that, too, until he found a message that said *I'm moving to Renaissance, a punk rock lady just showed up at the pub with cinnamon rolls,* with a photograph of what had to be at least fifty huge, fluffy, cream-cheese-covered cinnamon rolls in giant boxes on one of the pub tables.

'A punk rock lady' could only be Gwen. Bill jolted

out of bed and into the shower, holding one arm out so his phone didn't get wet as he texted her, *I thought you didn't get up until late!*

I lied, she wrote back after a minute, followed by winking and smiling emojis. *I thought you got up early!*

I usually do, he sent. *Slept in this morning, probably because somebody kept me up late at a concert. Showering now. Don't let everybody else eat the cinnamon rolls.* Then, aloud, he said, "Oh, God, everybody else. She's met the family without me. Oh my God," and put the phone down so he could hastily wash and get out of the shower.

There was another message from Gwen when he did: *Pix or it didn't happen.*

Still aloud, he said, "Uh," and texted back, *or what didn't happen?*

A shower, she wrote, and then a facepalm emoji followed. *OMG. I did not just ask a guy I've known like 19 hours for shower pix. Please ignore.*

As far as he could tell, Gwen Booker had been put on this earth in large part to make Bill blush. He wrote, *Too late, I'm already out,* then stared at himself in the mirror a moment. He *was* out of the shower, but not dressed, just wrapped in a towel. Aloud again, he said, "I'm not doing this," and then found out fast that he was actually terrible at taking 'hot shower guy' selfies. After about a dozen tries he got one he more or less liked, and without letting him think about it any more than that, sent it to Gwen with *This'll have to do.*

Response dots came up, went away, came up, went away, came up, went away, stayed away. Bill, concluding that the only correct thing to do was go die of mortification, went to get dressed with another blush staining his skin so deeply he could see it in his shoulders as he pulled a shirt on. He was just about dressed when his phone buzzed again. He picked it up so fast he fumbled it, dancing it across his hands before managing to get the screen on.

A series of gifs, starting with Blanche from the Golden Girls spritzing herself with water and eventually ending with the one of James McAvoy from *Wanted* fanning himself, rushed across his screen, followed by Gwen's *omfg,* and then a gif he didn't know with a bearded guy and text that said *I'll be in my bunk* across it.

There was really only one thing he could think of that that gif could mean, but he checked the internet anyway, and yes, that was what it meant. He wrote back with a devilish smiley face and a blush that Gwen responded to with a laugh and *I'd say you should've warned a girl, but God damn, Mr. Torben.*

Bill, feeling unreasonably pleased with himself, said, *I'll be there in a few minutes. Don't let them eat all the cinnamon rolls.*

She actually wrote back with ~~Baby, you can eat my cinnamo,~~ strike marks included, followed by *I mean, I'll make sure they'll share.*

Bill could not get to the pub fast enough.

For cinnamon rolls? his bear asked with a mix of curiosity and hope. *They're good for getting fat for winter.*

"Yeah," Bill answered through strangled laughter.

"Yeah, for cinnamon rolls. You and me, we're gonna win the Fat Bear Contest."

The bear gave a happy wriggle, which made it very hard for Bill not to wiggle happily along with it. He was still chuckling about it when he pulled up to the pub several minutes later. It wasn't open yet, but there were still seven cars in the parking lot, evidence that his parents had collected even more of the extended family overnight. Gwen's Impala was one of them, and the idea that she was in there with eight or twelve of his family members made Bill's stomach dip nervously. Although unless Jon had betrayed him, at least they didn't yet know that she was his fated mate. They *probably* wouldn't be regaling her with stories of his misspent youth, although the truth was, he'd been pretty clean-cut his whole life.

Cinnamon rolls, his bear reminded him, and Bill, chuckling again, got out of the truck to go get cinnamon rolls, and even more importantly, see Gwen. Only as he pushed the pub door open did he think he should have stopped for coffee, although a heartbeat later its scent hit his nose, so either someone had, or they'd broken out the staff's espresso machine from the back. They'd dragged a few tables together, taking up the middle of the room now, and a dozen people were shouting cheerfully, everybody trying to be heard over one another. Well-depleted boxes of cinnamon rolls had been broken down so they were mostly flat and kind of served as plates, even if that meant leaning forward, as one of his cousins was currently doing, to eat over the box so the crumbs didn't go everywhere.

Gwen, with her black, ragged hair and her rock star eyeliner, looked small, pale, and entirely at home in the midst of a bunch of enormous, blondish, golden-toned Torbens. She was sitting next to his mother, Heather, and his brothers were at opposite ends of the table, with their dad, Pete, across from Gwen at the middle. The rest of them were cousins and one uncle, who looked almost as much like their dad as Bill and his brothers did. One of them, Luke, glanced up, saw Bill, and roared a greeting that involved something about cool girls and cinnamon rolls. Everybody else joined in, although his mother, at least, got up to give him a hug and a kiss on the cheek, while Gwen, grin-deep in a cinnamon roll, waggled her eyebrows in greeting.

"Don't think we didn't see you sneak out last night," Heather murmured to Bill, but fondly. "Jon seems to think you were on a date with Ms. Booker, though, so I suppose I can forgive you."

"I've missed you too, Mom." Bill scooped her into a hug that made her squeak, although she otherwise patiently waited for her feet to be put back on the ground. To the assembly at large, he said, "Look, I know I got the musical booking wrong for the weekend, but honestly, we're scaring up a decent audience on our own. We didn't actually need the entire Torben clan to show up and fill out the ranks."

"She brought cinnamon rolls, my man," Luke said with intense sincerity. Bill had always thought he was the best-looking of the cousins, with wheat-blonde hair and a startling ocean blue gaze that defied all the other brown-eyed members of the family. "I'll show up anywhere there's cinnamon rolls."

"I'm impressed she brought so many you haven't eaten them all," Bill admitted, and flashed a smile toward Gwen. "Thanks."

"My pleasure." Her own ice-blue eyes were warm with smugness. "I figured fifty would be enough for up to twenty Torbens. They're *big* cinnamon rolls."

"You must've bought the bakery out of them," Bill's father said. He had a cup of coffee and the remains of one of the pastries in front of him, although his wife kept reaching across the table to steal bits of it.

"I left them with half a sheet and a great deal of confusion," Gwen confirmed. "They couldn't decide if they were thrilled to have moved them all in one sale or dismayed that they only had fifteen left for the rest of the day. You told me you played football, Bill, but you didn't tell me your entire family did. Was there anybody on your high school team who *wasn't* a Torben?"

"Danny Derwitz," his cousin Ashley said immediately. "He was the only guy on the team I could even conceivably date in high school. Everybody else was related to me."

Somebody threw a balled-up paper napkin at her. "That's not true!"

"No, but it's a good story." Ashley tossed a mane of tawny blonde hair over her shoulders as she grinned at Gwen. "Fortunately I was more interested in dating the cheerleaders. But yeah, no, there are a ton of us, but we're all spaced out just enough that there were usually a couple Torbens on both the varsity and JV teams. It's going to start all over again next year, too, because our cousin Rachel's oldest kid is hitting high school in the fall."

"It won't start all over again unless more of you have some children," Heather said with a sniff as she went back to the table. A whole hail of paper napkin balls rained down on her, and she batted them away. "Honestly, after all of you grew up with so many cousins, I'd think you would have started having kids years ago!"

"Maybe," Luke said dryly, "having so many cousins is why we *haven't.*"

Jon, down at the far end of the table, made a show out of looking significantly between Bill and Gwen, although to Bill's relief, no one else noticed. He knew what Jon meant, though. The truth was shifters often didn't have kids until they'd found their mates, because the hope of finding that one true love was always right there. So it was fate, not a clan-wide determination to deprive their parents of grandchildren, that kept most of them from having kids so far. And there was always the question of whether their partners would even want children, although Bill's mother liked kids so much he wasn't sure she could quite wrap her head around the idea that some people didn't.

His mother sniffed again, more pretend injury than actual pressure, and stole another bite of his dad's cinnamon roll. He looked amused, and Bill was suddenly certain he'd taken the one he had in front of him expressly so his wife *could* steal bites of it. That was true romance, he thought with a smile, although watching Gwen stuff half a cinnamon roll into her mouth, he wasn't certain it was the kind of true romance *she* wanted.

She wants 'shower pix,' his bear said. *I want cinnamon rolls!*

If I eat too many cinnamon rolls, she won't want shower pix anymore, Bill warned, and his bear looked at him skeptically.

Trust me. Your mate will always want shower pix. It sounded absolutely confident, even if it obviously had no idea what 'shower pix' were, and so Bill, grinning, sat down to have some cinnamon rolls.

CHAPTER 15

Gwen had not expected Bill to actually send her a shower pic. She could only thank her lucky stars that she'd gotten up to get coffee when that picture came in so that *his mother,* who was *sitting right next to her,* hadn't seen it.

After that, she counted her lucky stars that he'd sent it at all, because dear lord, that man was built. Not flawlessly chiseled like a film star, but big, strong, heavy muscle that looked like it came from hauling beer kegs around, not gym weights. His hair, dark brown when wet, had been slicked back and still dripping water down his incredibly wide shoulders, which looked a hundred times wider in the from-above selfie angle, and those deep brown eyes of his were alight with mischief. He'd been biting his lower lip, though, not a lot, just enough to suggest he was a little unsure of himself.

How anybody with that thick chest, huge arms, and delicious, lickable belly sliding into a low-wrapped towel could be unsure of himself, Gwen didn't know, but it made her like Bill Torben that much more, and she was already nursing a ridiculously powerful crush on the guy. Her heart actually skipped a beat when he came into the pub, and although it was no lie that his family were all good-looking people, she honestly could have been in the room alone with him, for all she cared about anybody else. His whole presence was warm and charming and reassuring, and she wanted to grab him, some cinnamon rolls, and go into the back office for some delicious downtime with him.

Down being the operative term. God damn. That towel had needed to be a little bit lower to satisfy Gwen's curiosity, or—ideally—just not on him at all. She was busy licking the frosting out of her cinnamon roll and staring at Bill when someone said something to her, emphatically enough that she thought they'd maybe spoken to her already. With a jolt, she put the cinnamon roll down and blinked at the—cousin, thank God it was a cousin and not his mother—on her left side. "Sorry, what?"

The cousin—this one was Ashley; the women were easier to keep track of, mostly because there were only three of them present—was grinning at her. Like, really, really grinning. She leaned in to say, "He's a really good guy. Super serious. I think you'd be good for him."

Ashley had obviously seen Gwen licking the cinnamon roll and staring at Bill. She wanted to be mortified, but instead laughed and screwed her face up in a squinch. "That obvious, huh?"

"The whole tongue thing there was kind of a give-away," Ashley said, wide-eyed with innocence. "Although he's gonna be real lucky if you're always that good with it."

Gwen clapped her hands over her face, laughing. "Gimme a cherry stem and I'll show you."

Ashley burst out laughing and knocked her shoulder against Gwen's. "Show *him*, girl, not me! Tell you what, you let me know what you need done around here for setup and I'll see if I can get all these huge lunks to do something useful while you make time with my cousin." As Gwen's eyebrows rose, Ashley spread her hands. "You're only here for the weekend, right? Gotta make hay while the sun shines. And no, I don't usually play wingman, but Bill really is a super good guy and he could use some time with a woman who watches him like he's a snack."

"A great big delicious snack," Gwen breathed, and Ashley smacked her hands together.

"See? That's what I'm talking about! Oh, shut up," she said to one of her cousins who was trying to over-hear. "I'm getting Gwen to tell me what needs to be done to make this off-beat gig tonight a sell-out tour, and you're going to help me do it. All of you are," she said, raising her voice firmly to the whole gathered family. "Luke, you and Jimmy can tend bar tonight, because you know they're going to need more help. Ruth and I will be backstage runners and help the musicians with whatever they need. And the rest of you, I'll give you something to do when I've got a list."

"Not me," the sole uncle—who might have been

Ashley's father, Gwen thought—announced. "I'm gonna sit around with the rest of the old folks and enjoy the show."

"Who are you calling old!" Heather said indignantly, and her husband, placidly, said, "Me. You remain in the bloom of freshness and youth, and always will."

Bill's mother rolled her eyes but also blew her husband a kiss, getting a sickly-sweet but also heartfelt "awww" from the gathered family. Gwen ducked her head, smiling at it all. She hadn't had a family life like this one. It was better not to dwell on that, but for a moment, she could at least feel envy and admiration. Luke, who was pop-star pretty, stuck his lower lip out as if pouting would get him his way. Gwen bet it often did, in fact, although none of his family looked moved by it as he said, "None of us will be able to do anything in half an hour. We'll all collapse of a carbs-and-sugar rush."

Gwen pointed at him. "*That* is why I got the cinnamon rolls with pecans and walnuts. *Protein.*"

He protested, "It's not enough protein to make a difference!" under his family's cheers and applause and mockery: clearly they were in fact used to him pouting his way out of doing things, and Gwen had apparently won favor by putting him in his place.

"What time's your band get here?" Ashley murmured.

"About two." Gwen looked at her phone like it would suddenly be almost two, although it couldn't be —and wasn't—much past ten.

Ashley beamed. "Perfect. Go do some important

marketing stuff with Bill." Above everybody else's chatter, she said, "All right, Gwen and Bill are heading out to put up flyers—I know, I know, totally retro, but it turns out people *do* still go to the mall and stuff—and the rest of us are going to get this place ship-shape for the concert tonight. They'll be back at two, 'cause that's when the Sixty Pix are supposed to be here. Bill, better take some cinnamon rolls for the road. You know, to keep your strength up."

Gwen made an undignified sound that was mostly drowned out by the others teasing Bill about not being able to go out and hang posters up without needing a rest, although Ashley heard it and gave Gwen an absolutely wicked smirk. Bill rose, a cinnamon roll in each hand and a look of faint confusion writ over his handsome face. Gwen stood, too, and shrugged a smile toward him. "I guess we've been given our marching orders. I've got the flyers in the car."

He said, "Oh good," in a completely befuddled tone, which was entirely reasonable, since Gwen did not, in fact, have flyers in the car.

Jon, though, sounded genuinely impressed. "You guys are a two-person marketing machine. If we had somebody with your level of get-up-and-go working for the Faire we'd make a killing. Instead I've got Laurie."

"*Hey!*" The youngest Torben brother, who had mostly been involved in his phone, looked up with an expression of credible injury. Gwen tilted her head toward the door, inviting Bill to escape with her, and they fled as the family began a debate about who did the most work around there, and whether anybody should take credit.

"I feel like I should stay here and defend you as the person who does the most work," Gwen said as they scurried out of the pub together.

"I am so sorry," Bill said in a rush. "I had no idea you'd be here so early. I never would have subjected you to them all alone. They're so much. And you only have my word for me being the one doing all the work."

She stopped as they reached her car, turned to him, and put her hand on his chest, which he couldn't object to because he still had a cinnamon roll in each hand and stopping her would require sacrificing at least one of them. With as much wide-eyed sincerity and trust as she could channel, she said, "But you wouldn't *lie* to me, would you, Bill?"

"Never," he said with such intensity that she felt bad about playing it up so much. "No. I'll never lie to you about anything, Gwen Booker." He brought his hands together to cup her face, prelude to a kiss that she wanted more than anything she had ever wanted in her whole weird life.

Except his hands were still full of cinnamon rolls, and instead of a kiss, Gwen got cream cheese frosting smooshed across her cheeks.

CHAPTER 16

*B*ill froze, which was the absolute worst thing he could do, because it meant he was standing there holding two cinnamon rolls against Gwen's face. But he couldn't make himself move, either, because in his mind he could hear the sticky *shluck!* of the cream cheese frosting releasing from her skin, and that somehow seemed worse than...than standing there framing her face with cinnamon rolls.

Oh, God, he whispered to his bear. *I don't think even fated mates can fix this.*

Gwen's gaze had softened as he'd spoken. Those ice blue eyes of hers had darkened into warm, welcoming pools, and he'd believed for a moment that he could really tell her anything, that she would love and accept him *exactly* as he was. She'd tipped her chin up, invitation for a kiss, and...

...he'd smeared cinnamon rolls all over her face.

He was fairly certain several thousand years had passed in the few seconds he'd been standing there, holding sticky pastries as he gazed down at her in absolute horror. Her eyes widened, then narrowed, and he waited for the inevitable slap, or knee to the nuts, or whatever the appropriately violent response to being cinnamon-rolled was.

Gwen *slithered* from between the cinnamon rolls as she doubled with laughter. Cream cheese slid through her hair. A blop of it fell from her hair to the ground, and her laughter rose into a helpless shriek before she fell back against the door of her car, absolutely *howling*. Tears ran down her face, smearing her eyeliner, so now she was both covered in frosting, cinnamon, and sad, dark clown streaks. She caught her breath, started to speak, looked up into his face, and dissolved into laughter again, clutching her arms around her belly as she shook with giggles. Eventually she gasped, "Oh my God. Oh my God," grabbed his shirt, and pulled herself upright to stand on her toes and kiss him.

She tasted like heaven and blessings and, inevitably, cinnamon-flavored cream cheese. She was also still laughing, and it ran through him like water, loosening some of his distress into an uncertain smile against her mouth. When she broke from the kiss, her eyes still bright with tears of laughter, he said, "I'm sorry," in a voice even he thought was small, and she threw her head back and laughed until she cried again.

"Don't be. Don't be. That was the best first kiss in the history of kisses. Oh, my God, that was amazing. 'How did you and Daddy meet, Mommy?' 'He shoved a cinnamon roll up my nose and I knew it was love.'" Gwen fell back against her car again, wiping her eyes as she giggled. "No, sorry, escalating, I know, big escalation there, just, oh my God. Your face. I have never seen a man's life pass before his eyes before. Ghosts would come to you for lessons on how to be white as a sheet. I thought you were going to throw up. And now you look like a fish out of water." A fresh bout of giggles swept over her.

She was right. Bill could feel his mouth opening and closing but he didn't seem to be able to stop it. He still had cinnamon rolls in his hands, for God's sake.

And Gwen Booker had just escalated their relationship in to 'Mommy, Daddy, love.'

He knew it was her amusement talking. That didn't stop his heart from clenching like someone had squeezed a fist around it, and he seem to have forgotten how to breathe. Weakly, as a protest that absolutely didn't help or even matter, he said, "I did not *shove* it up your *nose*," and Gwen sank to the ground, throwing her head against the car door as she laughed and laughed.

"Oh, God, you really are the best. You're just wonderful. No, you didn't, you smeared it all over my face, but never let the truth get in the way of a good story, big man. Oh, man." She wiped at her eyes again, less carefully, and came away with makeup smeared on her knuckles. "Oh, God, look at me. Okay, first stop before we go hang these non-existent flyers, we gotta go to my hotel so I can shower and fix my face."

"I don't know what to do with these cinnamon rolls," Bill said desperately.

It set Gwen off again, and he couldn't blame her. "Is

there a trash can out here? No way am I sending you back inside. They'd want to know what happened and then they'd tease you until the heat death of the universe, and we don't have time for that, so…how can a pub not have outdoors trash cans?" she added after glancing around.

"We do. They're just up on the deck."

"No, no, they'll see you if you go up there, too. Fine, get in the car." She crawled to her feet, still grinning hugely, and went around to open the passenger side door for him. "Don't get cream cheese all over the place, those seats are leather."

Bill sat carefully but froze again at that warning, feeling like a huge ungainly lunk. Gwen leaned in, murmured, "Safety first," and pressed right up against him as she buckled his seatbelt for him. Then from right there, she flashed another sudden bright and very wicked grin, almost against his mouth. "Oh, man, if it weren't daylight and in front of your actual family's pub, I could have a *real* good time with this."

The only thing that saved him from an instant raging erection was that only half the blood in his body flooded to his groin. The rest of it shot to his face, his blush hot enough that he thought it was actually melting the frosting on Gwen's cheeks. "Ooh," she murmured, still up close. "I think he likes it. Note to self: the big man might be into not being allowed to touch."

Then she withdrew, closed the car door firmly, and went around to the driver's seat while Bill was still trying to scrape enough brain cells together to decide what he thought of that idea. His blush was apparently fading, because his cock was getting harder, which seemed to be a solid answer to the proposal. He spluttered faintly as she slid into the car, and she gave him another bright, wicked grin. "Good news is the hotel is only a couple blocks away. You'll be able to throw those away in a minute. Although," she said, widening her eyes, "given that I'm covered in sticky white goo maybe you better hold on to them until we're in my room."

Bill slithered as far as he could down into the seat and groaned. "I *live* in this town."

"And when was the last time anybody gossiped about you? We'll give them a whole show this weekend," Gwen promised, and he was still trying to decide if that was a good or a bad thing when they got to her hotel.

To his relief, and her obvious huge amusement, there didn't happen to be anybody at the reception desk when they went in. He dumped the cinnamon rolls in the nearest trash can, blurting, "I can wait down here."

Gwen gave him a dubious look. "You could, but it'll be easier to clean up in my room. All the bathrooms in the lobby need keys, and the longer I stay down here the more likely somebody is to see me and get the wrong idea. Ah, there he goes, now." Bill was halfway to the elevators before she'd finished pointing out the flaws in his plan, and four floors later, she let him into what turned out to be a rather nice hotel suite. "Yeah," she said, watching him glance around in admiration, "you've put me up in style. And I appreciate it. Go wash your hands," she added with amusement, and he fled into the bathroom to do just that.

It took considerably more effort to get the sticky cinnamon roll residue off his hands than he expected, and their scent lingered despite the orange-sandalwood soap. He came out, hands dry but sniffable: his bear's nose was twitching and it was making him hungry. "That hotel soap smells amazing. Especially if you add cinnamon to it."

"Oooh, can I smell?" Gwen reached for his hand, then pulled hers back, looking embarrassed again. "I keep doing that. Sorry."

"You can touch me any time you want to. And, oh, God, that sounded better in my head."

Gwen laughed and did take his hand, bringing his knuckles to her nose and inhaling before she laughed again. "I think you're right, it does smell good, but mostly I can smell cream cheese and sugar. Cover me, I'm going in." She scooted past him to the bathroom while Bill stood there, frozen yet again as he tried to decide what 'cover me' meant in this situation.

Nothing, he told himself firmly. It was just a thing people said.

Blankets? His bear provided an image of them, warm and nestly in a den.

Bill relaxed with a chuckle. *Bears don't use blankets.*

*Bears **would** use blankets if they had them*, his bear informed him sternly, and Bill had to admit that seemed likely.

It also seemed likely that he should leave the room, go back down to the lobby and wait for Gwen there.

That was probably the polite thing to do. Except it also seemed a little weird to just not be there when she came out of the bathroom, and it seemed even weirder to yell, "I'm going downstairs!" over the sound of the running shower, like they were actually a couple or something.

His bear said, *You think too much,* which was very likely. *Sit down. Wait for our mate. Stop thinking!*

Bill suspected it was a bad idea to actually stop thinking, but, chastened, he made his way to the room's couch and sat, knowing he'd wait for Gwen Booker forever.

CHAPTER 17

Gwen turned the shower on as soon as she went in the bathroom, mostly because she didn't want Bill to think she was standing there gazing at herself in the mirror and thinking about the big gentle man in the main room. She looked ridiculous, anyway, with melted frosting dripped on her shirt and a thin glaze gleaming on her face. And her eyeliner had run when she'd laughed until she'd cried, which meant the new brand she'd picked up was cheap and needed to be thrown out.

That was a good thing to discover before she went on stage and sweated for two hours, actually. She cleaned her face with a makeup wipe—honestly, she'd had those in the car, but she hadn't thought of them, which would have been embarrassing if the whole thing hadn't been so funny. Once the worst of it, makeup and frosting alike, was gone, she stripped and got in the shower for the second time that morning, because getting sandwiched by cinnamon rolls was the kind of thing a person needed a complete do-over for.

Poor Bill's face had been priceless when he'd smooshed them all over her, too. She giggled again, hoping the shower muffled the sound, and scrubbed so she didn't give into the temptation to stand there in the hot water thinking about how he'd *blushed* at her no-hands suggestion in the car. The shower head had a good pulse setting. She had a few excellent ideas as to what to do with it while thinking about how she'd put her own hands to good use while Bill couldn't use his at all, buuuuuut that was entertainment for when he *wasn't* in the other room waiting for her. It only took a few minutes to get clean, and when she got out of the shower, wrapping her hair in one towel so she could dry off with the other, she realized he'd been right.

She also realized she hadn't brought any clothes to change *into* into the bathroom with her, so she went into the main room, wrapped in towels, to say, "You were right," as she went to her suitcase to find some-thing to wear. "The cinnamon and orange-sandalwood do smell amazing together."

"I. Oh. Sorry. Um." Bill stood abruptly and turned his back on her, his ears turning red. "Yes, they do. Sorry, I thought you'd be dressed."

"I forgot my clothes. You don't have to turn around," Gwen said, amused. "I didn't mean to make things awkward."

"As if coating you with cream cheese frosting didn't already do that."

Gwen grinned as she rooted through her suitcase.

"Hey, I know people who would pay good money for that kind of thing."

Bill flashed her a look over his shoulder. His ears were still red, but he asked, "Are you one of them?"

"Now why would I pay for it when I've got a big tall handsome guy who'll do it for free?" Gwen shot him a sideways grin, and swore his ears got even hotter. "No, okay, for real, I'm not so much into food sex. It's really sticky and prone to getting goop in places I don't want goop to be. You?"

"I can honestly say I've never even considered it," Bill replied faintly. "I take it you have. Unless you're guessing."

"Nope, not guessing, tried chocolate sauce and honey a couple of times, definitely not my thing. The cleanup is horrible, and I smelled like chocolate for two days. I smelled like honey, too, but that wasn't as annoying."

Bill mumbled something and sat back down on the couch, eyes fixed firmly on the floor. Gwen found a t-shirt that wasn't made entirely of wrinkles and tugged the towel off her head so she could pull the shirt on over the towel she wore wrapped under her armpits, then re-wrapped it at her waist. "What'd you say?"

"That you're out of my league."

A zing went through Gwen and she stopped looking for jeans, instead turning toward Bill. "Why on earth would you say that? You're kind, funny, and gorgeous."

"Also large and vanilla."

"Hey." Gwen went around the bed to sit on the

corner closest to Bill and leaned forward, elbows on her knees. "Do you know anything at all about actual vanilla?"

He raised his eyes, obviously startled. "It's boring?"

Gwen shook her head, smiling. "Vanilla is one of the world's most exotic flavors. It's the only edible orchid flower, and real vanilla is so expensive because the orchids have to be hand-pollinated. It's been in high demand for over five hundred years for the delicacy of its flavor and scent, for food and perfumes. We only think it's common because we have access to imitation vanilla and practically no sense of what it takes to acquire the real stuff. There's a reason it's the most popular ice cream, big man. There's nothing in the whole world like vanilla."

Bill's eyebrows furrowed and a funny little smile came over his face. "Why do you even know that?"

"I had to do a report on a common food for my teacher when I was a teenager," Gwen said with a grin. "I thought vanilla would be easy. It turned out I was wrong. I learned so much about it. I won't bore you with any more details, but let me leave you with the fact that it was Queen Elizabeth the First who popularized it in Europe after it was brought back to her as a gift from the New World."

"I had no idea."

"Well, I did, so don't try to tell me how boring you are by claiming to be vanilla. The way I see it that means you're probably full of subtlety and depth." She reached out toward him without thinking, and to her surprise, he met her touch with his own fingertips.

It felt like an actual electric spark jolted through her at that light touch. It stung through her whole body, hardening her nipples and making Gwen very aware she hadn't put a bra on, and pooling heat between her thighs. A little breath escaped her, and even more to her surprise, Bill curled his fingers, catching hers with his and drawing her toward him just the littlest bit. She went willingly, a few awkward steps at the odd angle they were connected at, and then thumping to her knees in front of him. He brushed his fingers up her arm, ghost-light, and framed her face with that same barely-there touch before bringing his mouth to hers.

Their lips barely brushed in the most tentative question before he closed the distance again with more certainty. He tasted like cinnamon and coffee, and his beard was long enough to not scruff, though it tickled a little, making her laugh. She felt his smile against her mouth in return. "The beard's got to go?"

"Jury's out. Kiss me again while I think about it."

Bill chuckled and slid his hands to her waist, pulling her up. *Effortlessly* pulling her up, and lifting her into his lap once he had a solid grip. The towel wrapped around her waist wasn't meant to stand up to that kind of treatment, and fell loose to her hips, one thigh exposed where the ends of the towel opened, the other hidden beneath its pooled cloth. There was *just* enough of it that she wasn't suddenly mostly naked in Bill's lap —the cloth crumpled and covered the relevant bits, but only barely—and Bill, in a very gentlemanly fashion, neatly tucked it around her so she was in less danger of exposing everything.

She still felt incredibly undressed and meltingly hot with it, sitting across his lap like that. His hands came back to her waist, fingers partially on her t-shirt, partially against her skin. He was so *warm*, and so big, and so confident. She whispered, "Thank you," and he grinned ruefully from up close.

"Not that I didn't like the towel's idea of getting out of the way, but I think that should be your decision, not a towel's." He lifted his hands to her face again, framing her cheeks carefully, and murmured, "I think you said something about another kiss?"

"I did, yeah."

"Lemme work on that, then." He nuzzled at her mouth, making her breathe a laugh, and his lips touched hers, gentle, exploratory, and then as she answered eagerly, with greater hunger and command, until Gwen thought she could drown in that kiss. She slid her hands over his shoulders, into his hair, and he groaned, a soft delicious sound before moving his hands to the small of her back and tugging her closer. He was so big, but they fit together so *well*, and he made her laugh. Casting caution to the wind suddenly seemed like a great idea.

Gwen took his hand and slipped it under her shirt in invitation. Bill groaned again, sliding his fingers upward until he cupped her breast, big fingers playing lightly with her nipple and making her shiver and arch with appreciation. Then he groaned from the bottom of his soul and moved his hand back down, mumbling, "Wait. Wait." Both of his hands went to her hips, over the damp towel, and he set her back a few inches as he caught his breath. "I'm sorry. I don't want to stop, but there's something I want to—think I need to—tell you before we go any farther."

Incredible disappointment crashed through Gwen, so powerful it made her flush a deep ruddy red she could feel it burn all the way past her collarbones. She slumped, eyes closed, and shook her head. This had happened more times than she could count, and it never stopped sucking. "I know what you're going to say."

"I—*what?*" Bill sounded so completely astounded that Gwen made herself open her eyes to meet his thunderstruck expression. "You do? *How?*"

"It happens all the fucking time." Gwen climbed out of his lap, knotting the towel around her waist again and returning to the edge of the bed to sit despondently. "'Gwen, you're great, I really like you, but look, I think you should probably know that I've had a crush on you since I was nine. This is my dream come true. You're the stuff of my fantasies.' I mean, at least you have the decency to say it now instead of after we've gone to bed together. Most guys don't do it until they've woken up with Rita."

Bill, his voice utterly bewildered, said, "Rita?"

"You know," Gwen said miserably. "Rita Hayworth. Everybody wanted to go to bed with Gilda, that's what she said. Her most famous character. They were always disappointed when they woke up with Rita."

"I...Rita Hayworth...wasn't she incredibly beautiful? What kind of idiot...never mind. What are you talking about? What—are you...Rita Hayworth?" Bill sat up, adjusting his jeans, then spread his hands in confusion. "I mean...are you famous? I already know you're famous! You're Gwen Booker! What are you talking about?"

A whole new sinking sensation opened in Gwen's chest and drained through her in an awful chill. "Are you serious?"

"Of course I'm serious. What am I missing here? Who am I supposed to be thinking you are?"

Gwen closed her eyes. For once in her life, she'd found somebody who really wasn't haunted by her history, maybe, and here she was, revealing it all to him. After a minute, instead of answering out loud, she got up and found her phone, did an image search, and handed it to him.

That let her watch the whole process of realization march across his face. Confusion again at first, at the pictures of a pretty little girl, then a pretty young woman with pale blue eyes and hair so fair it was nearly white. She smiled, that kid did. Such a big wide smile for the cameras. Gwen still had that same smile, but it played differently slashed with deep red lipstick instead of soft pink.

Same with the big blue eyes. The color was unmistakable, but with the harsh eyeliner she usually wore, the look was completely different from what the studios had called the 'Paul Newman Effect' when they'd first discovered her. People could drown in those eyes, clear as the sea. Fall all the way into them. Gwen watched Bill glance from the pictures to her, specifically at her eyes, and then she saw understanding and realization start to drop into place. "You're Emma Hart. From the..." He faltered, then shook his head. "I don't remember the show. There were a bunch of you. The New Kidz Club, something like that, I remember that. It was supposed to be a rival to...I forget what the mouse kids were called, too."

"Yeah." Gwen sat back down, putting her face in her hands. "I'm Emma Hart. Or I was. Gwen Booker is my real name, but they didn't think it was cute enough."

"You were..." Bill paused again, clearly trying to collect his thoughts. "You were *really* famous. You were the most successful of them, weren't you?"

"That depends on how you define success." Gwen found she couldn't stay still after all, and rose to get underwear and her jeans, which she snaked on under the towel before dropping it and looking for socks. "Did I get the lead role in *Starting School*? Yeah."

Beneath that, Bill said, "That's it, that was the show," but it wasn't an interruption, just him placing her history. Gwen came over to get her phone and walked away again, still unable to stop moving. "Did I get my own show after that? Yeah. And then a bunch of movies for the network, and a couple real ones, and a record deal, because hoo boy, my dad, he sure could manage a tweenage-to-teenager's career. I skyrocketed. I was the next big thing, but I was terrified. And when I said I didn't want to do the record, Dad said I had to because I'd signed the contract. So I did the worst job I possibly could, and the day the album released, my dad and all the money I'd earned since I was nine years old disappeared."

She'd been living with that story for almost fifteen years. It almost surprised her that she could still be so *angry* about it. "Nobody cared," she said to the window, or the wall, or anybody but the big kind man in the room, the one who hadn't known who she was until she blew it by telling him. "Not one person I'd grown up with, none of the other parents, *definitely* not the studio heads, they didn't care. They told me I could still be big, all I had to do was sign on the dotted line. Yeah, because that worked out so well for me. I spent almost my entire childhood in the spotlight and I had nothing except a bunch of lunatic fans who thought I was their dream girl to show for it. I told the studios to fuck off and walked away. That worked out great, too, mind you, because what the hell did I know about dealing with the real world after growing up on set?"

"I am so sorry." Bill's voice was gentle, still not an interruption.

The way he said it helped, somehow. Maybe just because she felt listened to. Gwen turned back to him, finding his expression a strange combination of crestfallen and fiercely protective. It almost made her smile. "It's not your fault."

"No. But I'm sorry. So what did you do?"

Gwen exhaled and went to sit in the chair across from him. "I cut off all my hair and dyed what was left black and started wearing different clothes and makeup. And joined a rock band when I realized I hated not making music as much as I'd hated being famous on somebody else's terms. You really didn't know?"

"I really didn't. I can see it now, especially because you're not wearing makeup, but you grew up." Bill smiled crookedly. "I wouldn't have guessed that cute baby face would turn into those razor cheekbones. But I never would have even imagined it. Can I ask you something?"

"If it's, 'did he ever turn up again with my money?' the answer is no. I haven't seen him since I was eighteen. I hope he went and got a new identity and then got killed in a car wreck so he didn't have a chance to spend any of it."

Bill nodded without a hint of judgment. "That's what I was going to ask, yeah." He hesitated. "Your mom?"

"Aaaah, my mom wanted to be famous. She would take me to local auditions when I was little. That's about all I remember about her. She died of a drug overdose when I was five."

Bill, involuntarily, said, "Jesus," and despite herself, Gwen let go a short laugh.

"I know, right? I got the whole child star tragic backstory, didn't I? It was actually a medical error, my Dad sued the hospital and moved us to Hollywood with the money, but I only ever heard him say it that way, that she died of a drug overdose. I didn't even know what had really happened until I looked it up when I was an adult. So now you know the whole sordid truth about Gwen Booker."

"I sincerely doubt that." Bill sounded so earnest it made Gwen smile again, which didn't happen often when she talked about her past. He went on, "I mean,

I'm glad you told me, because it would have been embarrassing to have a tabloid cover our wedding or something and only find out then, but for what it's worth, I don't want to go to bed with Gilda. I really like Gwen."

Gwen closed her eyes, basking in the warmth the quiet words surrounded her with. "That's one of the nicest things anybody's ever said to me." Then she opened her eyes again, smiling. "Wedding, though?"

"You started it with the cinnamon roll," Bill said calmly. "'How did you and Daddy meet?' You don't think I'm the kind of guy who goes around having children out of wedlock, do you?"

A real laugh rolled through Gwen this time, even though it was quiet. "I don't think people who use the term 'wedlock' in this day and age do that, no."

"There we go, then. Now, look, I don't know if you've actually got flyers to put up, but it's past eleven now and if we're going to paper the city in advertisements, you'd better go put on your superhero disguise so we can head out."

"It works, doesn't it? The dark eyeliner and the red lipstick? I look like somebody else. Enough of the time, anyway."

"You look like a rock star," Bill murmured, and Gwen, unexpectedly happy, went to put on her makeup.

CHAPTER 18

hat had not gone as planned.

Bill was still looking at pictures of 'Emma Hart'—on his own phone now, since Gwen had taken hers back—when she came out of the bathroom with her makeup applied, but when he glanced up to see if he saw the child star in the rock musician, it turned out that all he really saw was his fated mate. She was strong and gorgeous and had been through far more than he'd ever imagined, and come out as this incredible woman he was clearly destined to fall wildly in love with.

And he had completely failed to tell her he was a shifter.

"Gwen—"

"So I emailed—oh. Yes?" Gwen stopped her burst of enthusiastic speech that ran over his, her pale eyes carefully bright. It was as if she'd applied armor as well as the makeup. She'd almost said as much, talking about how she'd cut her hair, dyed it, and learned whole different makeup styles from what she'd been like as a kid. He thought about her 'Day Job Gwen' picture on her driver's license, and how even that woman was a far cry from the waif of a girl she'd been famous as. It was *all* armor, in its way, and the last thing Bill wanted was to give her another reason to get defensive now. It would be one thing if he had some idea of how she'd react to learning his secret, but even though his bear—and every shifter he knew who'd found their mate—said it would be *fine*, trusting that in the moment was much scarier than Bill had imagined.

"You go first," he said with a smile. "You're in there doing double duty getting makeup on and emailing people while I'm out here twiddling my thumbs, so hit me up."

She laughed, which was good. Maybe she wasn't too upset about confessing *her* secrets to him. "I emailed a poster over to the print shop in town and asked for a rush job. It turns out my new friend Ripley works there during the day, so by the time we get over there, they should have a hot stack of flyers ready for us to paper Renaissance with."

"I'm half afraid we're going to end up with a crowd too big for the pub," Bill confessed.

Gwen tossed her hair, which she'd dried into the same kind of spiky ponytail she'd been wearing yesterday, and sparkled those amazing eyes at him. "Then I guess I'll have to come back to play Renaissance again. I'm not busy next weekend."

Bill's heart lurched so hard he stood up like he couldn't contain the feeling. Then he felt silly for the sudden motion, and couldn't figure out what to do with himself. He managed to say, "Don't tempt me. I could book you every weekend for a year and not get enough of you."

Her eyebrows quirked and a funny little smile, almost like a question, formed on her lips before she glanced down, shrugged a bit, and glanced back up at him. "Only weekends?"

"I didn't want to presume?" He wanted to do much, much more than presume, and he wanted it all to start like they'd begun on the couch, but he still couldn't figure out how to blurt 'by the way, sometimes I'm a bear' without sounding like a complete lunatic.

Shift, his bear said mellowly. *That'll prove it.*

That would scare her! And bears don't fit in hotel rooms very well!

How do you know? the bear asked curiously. *We've never shifted in one before.*

That was true, and made Bill chuckle despite his feeling of awkwardness. *Trust me. We'd knock over the coffee table, and probably shred the furniture.*

The bear looked around, and allowed that the coffee table, at least, seemed like it would be endangered. *Let's go to the woods, then.*

There was no way the bear would really understand why large human men didn't suggest taking small—or medium or large, for that matter—human women into the woods less than a day after meeting them. *You'll just have to trust me,* he said again. *That kind of thing doesn't seem as great to humans as it does to bears.*

A mighty sigh met this remark, but the bear settled down, and Bill discovered Gwen was at the door, waiting for him with a look of amusement. He wondered if she would still be amused if she found out he was debating a bear, and then thought *he* would think that was hysterical.

"Come on," Gwen said. "We have flyers to pick up. And…a year might be a little presumptuous."

He scrambled through his thoughts as he followed her out of the hotel, trying to remember what he'd said before the bear interrupted, and then hope flew through him. "Next weekend, then? Whether you want to play at the pub or not?"

"Yeah," she said with an almost shy smile. "I'd like to spend some time with you when we're *not* running around trying to make a gig happen."

"It's a date," Bill promised fervently. If he didn't have to explain everything this weekend, he was sure he could figure it out. "Although I can't believe you want to spend any time with me at all after being introduced to half my family."

"Oh, no." Gwen's eyes were bright. "No, they're honestly great, Bill. I told you what my family was like. So many of you getting along so well? It's wonderful. And I like your cousin Ashley. She plays hardball."

Bill laughed as they left the hotel. "Yeah, she does. She used to keep the younger cousins in line. Still does, I guess. She's about ten years younger than me, but I think Laurie and Jon actually live in fear of her."

"As well they should." They did an awkward little dance at her car that ended in Gwen dangling the keys at him. "It's chivalrous and everything for you to want to open the door for me, but I've got the keys, so get out of the way." He did, sheepishly, and Gwen opened her door and crawled in to open his from the inside, calling, "Oooh, it still smells like cinnamon. That's my new favorite scent. Okay, where's this print shop?"

"On Second and Main," Bill said as blandly as he could after he'd gotten in the car. Gwen gave him a hard stare and he laughed. "Oh, you meant how do we get there? Left out of the parking lot, right after three blocks, I'll navigate more from there."

"Hnf. Thank you, Mr Bad Jokes Man."

Bill sketched a bow. "You're welcome. It's not far. Nothing's far, in Renaissance."

"I like it. And the setting couldn't be more perfect." Gwen nodded toward the mountains that soared up more or less a stone's throw away. "I assume this is a real skiing hotspot?"

"Summer tourism is the Ren Faire, winter tourism is skiing." Bill pointed out their next turn. "I don't do either."

Gwen laughed. "No? No skiing? Why not?"

The real answer was that in his heart, Bill was certain if he had a fall, he would instinctively shift into a bear, which was better at rolling through snow than he was. That didn't seem like an answer he could offer right now, so he said, "Two hundred and forty pounds of me hurtling downhill at high speed has always seemed like a bad idea," which was also true.

"I've never been either. We can go try the, what do they call it? Bunny hills? Do they really call them that? Sometime."

"I don't know if they really call them that, but what

if I counter-proposed just going up to the resorts and watching the skiers from the nice safe warmth of the ski lodges while drinking hot chocolate?"

"Hmph. Where's your sense of adventure?"

"I'm not sure I have one," Bill admitted. "Turn right here, and we're there."

"Oh, that was fast. I bet they're not ready yet." Gwen swung out of the car and looked the little strip mall up and down. "This is totally Anywhere, USA, isn't it? I like it, though. And all the storefronts are full. It seems like Renaissance is kind of thriving."

"It's a—" Bill broke off, abruptly at a loss. Renaissance was a shifter town, which meant shifters from all walks of life had settled there, knowing they had a relatively safe community, a lot of wilderness next door, and a good reason to keep the town bustling and alive. But he couldn't say that without explaining shifters, and while there *was* a scruffy patch of trees over to the left of the strip mall, he didn't think it was quite private enough to change into a 1200 pound grizzly bear in. He ended up saying, "—a good little town," awkwardly, although Gwen didn't seem to notice the awkwardness.

"I've never lived anywhere this small. Not for long, anyway. We lived in Seattle when I was little, and then it was Los Angeles until everything went to hell. It took me a while to settle in Denver but I didn't really *live* anywhere between then." At Bill's questioning look, Gwen shrugged. "I did do the van life for a while. I didn't want to stay anywhere that people might recognize me, so I basically avoided them entirely for a couple of years and just drove all over the place. Did some street busking to make money, or picked up odd jobs in towns I was going through. I was terrible at everything except, like, raking leaves. Eventually I'd, you know, gotten enough older, lost enough baby face, that I didn't look as much like myself, and I got a secret weapon to disguise myself."

"A secret weapon…?"

She whipped out a pair of glasses from a pocket and put them on with great flair. They were thick-framed cat-eyes with sparkles, and did something to the color of her eyes. "Wow," Bill said after a moment of studying her. "Those really don't suit you at all."

Gwen laughed, clearly delighted. "They really don't, do they? But they're incredibly distracting."

"Are the lenses tinted? Your eyes look almost green."

"Yup. Just a little yellow in them. No rose-colored glasses for me. Also they get darker outside—" They did as she was talking, a polarizing effect taking place. "—so it's extra-disguisey, or something. It's less of an issue now," she added, taking the glasses off. "But it helped a lot when I was in my early twenties. Psycho-logically, at least."

"I imagine so. That must have been difficult." It felt like a completely inadequate thing to say, but Gwen's smile turned soft and grateful.

"It was bad the first few years. I like being Gwen Booker, though, once I got used to it. She's got a lot more freedom than Emma Hart ever would have had. She also has a gig to sell out, so why don't we go see if those flyers are ready, and tell everybody there's a party tonight?"

"Yes, ma'am." Bill saluted. They went in to collect the flyers, and came out again trying desperately not to laugh at how Ripley had played it *totally* cool, like, yeah, they knew Gwen Booker, hey Gwen, nice to see you, in front of their coworkers, only for bone-piercing shrieks and giggles to break just before the door closed behind Bill and Gwen again. "Are you sure you're not top of the charts?" Bill demanded as they got back in the car. "You seem awfully popular!"

"If I had a major label behind me for the next album I'd go stratospheric," Gwen said with charming frankness. "That might sound arrogant, but the band's put the work in over the past decade. The thing—*a* thing—is that labels don't want workhorses. They want you to be a hit with the first album these days, instead of building an audience over two or three albums and breaking out. We've built the audience. If things were a little different, we'd break out."

"Do you want to? If we go over a couple blocks we'll be downtown and can put flyers up there. This area doesn't get as much foot traffic."

"Okay." Gwen drove them over, her expression thoughtful, but she didn't answer the question until they were out of the car in the cool autumn morning and hanging up posters. "If I personally get any more famous than I am, everybody's going to remember Emma Hart, and that's not my fave, no. I mean, a lot of my fans already know, but they've, like, let it go? But it'd become *the* story about the band. On the other hand..." She shrugged as they walked around, sticking posters to light poles and going into businesses to ask if they could put them up there. "The band *has* put in the work. I'd love to see them get the recognition they deserve. Even though they'd also get overshadowed by who I used to be."

"I take it they all know?"

"Yeah. But knowing, and being in the middle of a media shitstorm about it, are not the same things. Trust me," she said wryly. "*I* know."

"I bet you do. Is this what you do?" He nodded toward the flyers they'd just posted. "I mean, is it how you built your audience?"

"Some of it. Penny, she's my drummer, she's amazing at social media. I stay away from it, obviously, but Penny's out there with the videos and the clips and the quips, and because I'm only like a background character in them in a lot of ways, the rest of them have gotten a chance to shine. I've lost most of the band to bigger names over the years, because of her promo, but we've found great new people the same way. And she's stuck with me. She says she wants to be the one who was there all along when Sixty Pix breaks big."

"What's with the name? 'Sixty Pix?'"

Gwen grinned, a big bright flash of teeth. "That's actually Penny, too. Well, it's us, but she was looking for a good hashtag to promote her stage photography and landed on this idea of posting sixty pictures a week, ten a day except on Mondays. Her tag was 'Sixty Pics,' P-I-C-S instead of P-I-X, but when the band started to actually take shape we thought we could use that, so for a while it was Sixty Pics of Sixty Pix, and at some point she dropped the P-I-C-S spelling and here we are. My drummer, the marketing whiz kid."

"She sounds great. It'll be nice to meet her."

"Speaking of which." Gwen took her phone out to check the time, then waggled it at him. "We should grab a snack and go back to the pub. The band will be there soon."

CHAPTER 19

*B*ill Torben was the only guy Gwen had met in years—maybe ever—who'd learned she used to be Emma Hart, absorbed that information, and then just didn't seem to care very much. He asked questions like he was interested in her, but not like he was desperate to find out all the dirt on being a child star, or like it changed what he thought of her.

It was weird, Gwen thought, and it was *wonderful.* She hadn't told anybody but Penny, over years, as much about herself as she'd told Bill in a few hours. She could hardly believe how easy and comfortable it was. Or how much fun she'd had, just wandering around downtown Renaissance putting up posters with him.

The town really was a lovely little place, snugged right up against the mountains. Bill had mentioned it would start snowing pretty soon, but that they usually got through Oktoberfest without the white stuff. The whole place had an old-timey old-west feel to it, with the tallest buildings being maybe four stories, but those were mostly church steeples or statuary on top of government buildings. It was all mostly stonework, not wood like she actually thought of the Old West, although that idea was probably from movies rather than towns that had survived the gold rushes and railroads coming in. The streets were unexpectedly wide, and traffic was surprisingly limited, which Bill had waved off with a pass of his hand. "It's the whole Colorado outdoors lifestyle thing, only moreso for Renaissance. Pedestrians and cyclists get priority. There's a stoplight you have to wait at for almost five minutes over in front of the courthouse. Other places have statement sculptures. Renaissance has a statement stoplight."

Gwen had burst out laughing. "That's incredible."

"It makes everybody mad, including locals," Bill had replied with a grin. "Most of us learn not to drive on Court Street at all, and tourists get a *lot* of tickets there. And since it and Main Street are the main streets, it cuts way, way down on traffic."

There was an airport that catered to the winter tourist season, but of course, ran year 'round with flights to the West Coast and as far east as Chicago and Atlanta. A girl could get to most major cities for gigs from here, if she really needed to. And, although she'd driven, there was a new high-speed train that went from there to Denver, and she could get anywhere in the world from Denver.

Not that Gwen was thinking about moving to Renaissance. That would be ridiculous.

But it *was* awfully pretty, and she could obviously

drop by the Harlequin to play any time she felt like it, and—and Gwen Booker was smart enough not to throw her entire life over for some guy. At this stage of the game she was, at least. For sure. Definitely. She'd learned her lesson on that front at least three times, and in her grimmer moments recognized that there was probably some kind of pattern there that involved her horrible father and bad decisions regarding men.

Bill really didn't seem like a bad-decision kind of man, though. He practically had 'responsibility' written all over him, given how seriously he took running his family's business, and how frustrated he was with his younger brothers' lackadaisical attitude toward it.

He was the kind of man who would tell her moving to Renaissance so she could snuggle up to his huge, safe self some more was an unwise decision. Dammit.

Gwen breathed, "Hold your horses, girl," under her breath to herself. They had plans for a not-gig-related get-to-know-you weekend the next weekend. That was far enough in advance to be planning stuff for a guy she met yesterday.

Bill, who apparently had amazing hearing, said, "Horse girl?" in an odd tone, and Gwen laughed as they headed back to her car.

"Not really. I haven't ridden since I was a teenager, and I only did then for work. I liked it, though. You?"

"I think it would be cruel and unusual punishment to make a horse carry a guy my size. And they don't like how I smell."

"Really?" Without thinking about it, Gwen leaned over to give him a sniff after they'd both gotten in the car. He still smelled as nice as he had the night before, with the hint of cinnamon fading. "I think you smell nice."

He looked down at her with her nose on his shoulder, fighting off a grin. "Well, thank you."

Gwen sat up again, trying to find some shred of dignity. "I'm not weird."

Bill totally lost the battle with his grin and went straight into a peal of laughter. "Glad to hear it. Let's go home, weirdo."

Gwen's heart gave another silly jump at the word *home*, although she told herself, very sternly, that Bill certainly didn't mean it that way. His home, maybe, more or less, but not *hers*. Still, she felt bubbly inside, and the drive back to the pub was a quick one filled with more light-hearted chat. Pulling up, she saw Penny's van, and yowled in dismay. "They got here before us! Oh, but only just, okay, that's fine."

The rest of her band members were in fact just piling out of the van. Penny, a firecracker of a drummer at five foot five; Myles, the lanky bass player almost as tall as Bill who towered above her, Gemma, the keyboardist, and Sandy, who played guitar. Penny waved at the Impala, shouted a greeting, and widened her eyes when Bill got out the passenger door, her gaze darting back and forth between Gwen and the big man with interest. "This is Bill Torben," Gwen called. "He's the owner. We've been out flyering the town!"

"Uh huh." Penny, still wide-eyed, came over to shake Bill's hand. She was a full foot shorter than he was even in her boots, and made entirely of curves and red hair. "Nice to meet you, Bill. I'm Penny, the drummer."

Bill's hand, which enveloped even Gwen's, swallowed half of Penny's arm. He was a little wide-eyed, too, shaking her hand. "Nice to meet you too. Welcome to Renaissance and the Thunder Bear Brewpub."

"Thanks. Those are Myles, Sandy, and Gemma. I hope you've got a lot of beer ready, because our socials are actually going nuts." She turned to Gwen, all business. "We had people coming in anyway, you know that, but with this 'OMG potential disaster' thing, they're frickin' *rallying*, G. I got people posting road trip pics from all over the western half of the country. We got some folks coming down from *Edmonton*."

"In a car?" Gwen asked in horrified appreciation. "That's a full day's drive! I mean, a twenty-four hour day!"

"In a car," Penny confirmed. "They left last night and are driving in shifts. Planning to be here by tonight. We better put on a hell of a show."

Sandy, who sang a tenor second lead as well as playing guitar, called, "We always do," in an alto much lighter than her singing voice. Myles put a laconic thumb into the air, and Gwen ended up beaming at her bandmates.

"Yeah, we do. Okay, Bill, do you mind if we just kind of do our thing for a while? We'll want to get set up and make sure the sound system is all working."

"I brought the screens," Penny said in a significant tone.

Gwen paused, looking from her to the van and back again. "Really? You think it's going to go that well?"

"Babe, you got two new songs from our album going viral and promised four more over the weekend, which, thank you very much you might have *warned* us about, and you sent up a bat-signal-distress-call. People are *loving* this. Yeah, I think it's going to go this well."

"Viral?" Gwen's voice rose. "I didn't film them or anything?"

"My *dude*," Penny said in a voice she reserved for when Gwen was being particularly dim, "*you* didn't have to film it. The audience at the Harlequin last night did."

Gwen stared at her. "But I don't want to go viral. That's what you're there for."

"You're the only lead singer in the entire universe who actually wants the rest of the band to get more face time than them, you know that, right? If you didn't want to go viral, you shouldn't have played two new songs in front of three hundred people the day you asked your fans to come save your ass because of a mess-up with the booking. No offense," Penny said to Bill, crisply.

"None taken. This is the most interesting mistake I've ever made. But...screens?" The big man sounded a bit lost.

"Fortunately you've got a big parking lot here," Penny said, as if that cleared everything up. "You're going to need somebody to police the actual parking, because we'll be putting the screens up probably..." She turned, examining the parking lot, then waving. "There and there. Maybe there, too. And there. I brought six," she told Gwen, turning all the way around to get back to her.

"I'm sorry," Bill said slowly. "Are you suggesting you think there's going to be overflow audience?"

"Have you checked your ticket sales?"

"No, I..." Bill trailed off, staring at the petite drummer, than got his phone out and scrolled through it, paling. "What the hell? The pub—the code—we're not fire-coded for this many people! Not even with the beer gardens!"

"Hence the screens," Penny said patiently. "You might need to put a cap on sales. Keep some for the door, but I think most of our fans who are coming from out of town have gotten their tickets already, so we shouldn't have to turn anybody away. That would be crushing. Bad PR. Can't let that happen. I'll make sure to put the word out about buying them in advance, though, to make sure of not being disappointed."

Bill said, "Screens?" again, and this time Penny, shaking her head, yelled for Myles to get one. He eyed her, but ambled into the van and came out again with a rolled-up screen about two feet taller than he was. Sandy hurried over to help him unroll it, then waved at Bill through its incredibly thin material. The whole thing was probably eight by twelve, not exactly jumbo, but pretty flipping big for something that could be rolled up and put in a van. Bill made a spluttering noise, and Penny gave him a serene smile as he said, "Is that even *real?*"

"Myles's company is developing them. They're insanely cool and we get to stress-test them. Look, I'm sorry," she said to Bill, "but I've really got to take Gwen away and us get this all set up so we're sure we can be seen inside and out tonight. We brought the outdoors sound system stuff, too," she said to Gwen.

"Where did you put the *band* if all that was in your van?"

"I tied them to the roof. No, Myles drove, too. We couldn't make it work otherwise. First thing I'm buying when we hit it big is a tour bus, G. This trying to Tetris everything and everybody into the van sucks."

"I'll *buy* you a tour bus when we hit it big," Gwen promised. "All right, it looks like we've got some real work to do. Bill, is it okay if we prop the doors open so we can tromp in and out?"

"Yeah, of course. I'll tell the staff—and my family—to stay out of the way, or better yet, be helpful if they can be." He gave Gwen a wide-eyed smile. "You have no idea how impressed I am. And also slightly terrified. This has been the most overwhelming twenty-four hours of my life."

"So far."

He stared at her, then laughed. "Yeah. If you're going to stay in it, yes, definitely, so far. Nice to meet you, Penny. I'm going to go tell everybody to take their marching orders from you."

Penny said, "Oh, I like him," approvingly as he

walked away, and then, as soon as he was out of earshot, elbowed Gwen. "Eeeehhhhh?"

Gwen hunched her shoulders, trying not to grin. "'Eeeehhhhh,' what?"

"He's hot! He's huge! Are you into him?"

"What do you mean, he's hot? He's one hundred percent not your type!"

Penny gripped both Gwen's shoulders, looking up into her eyes. "Babe, I don't need to be into guys to aesthetically appreciate huge hotness in one. And you *are* into him, or you wouldn't be prevaricating."

"Oh, I'm prevaricating, am I? What the hell is prevaricating?"

"Avoiding the question."

"Oh." Gwen hunched her shoulders again. "I guess I'm prevaricating, then, yeah. Yes, he's hot, and yes, I'd hit that like a gong. In fact, I almost did earlier, except I —" She broke off, frowning after Bill. "He put the brakes on, actually. He said he had something to tell me and I figured it was, you know, he recognized me and all that, except it wasn't that, so I confessed my entire stupid history and he never did tell me what he wanted to say."

"Oooh." Penny's eyebrows rose and she, too, swung to look after Bill. "I bet he wanted to tell you he'd fallen in love with you at first sight and you were meant to be together, but since you derailed that, how'd he take it? The whole sordid past thing?"

"He thought my dad sucked."

Penny nodded, waited, then blinked back at Gwen. "That's it?"

"Pretty much."

"Oh." The drummer's smile bloomed. "Oh, yeah, I *do* like him. Awesome. Hang on to that one, G. He's a good 'un. But not until after we're done setting up, because O. M. G. do we have a lot of work to do."

CHAPTER 20

*B*ill, having three younger brothers and a whole load of younger cousins, knew organized chaos when he saw it, but the Sixty Pix had it down to an art form. Tall slender Myles and the square-jawed pianist, Gemma, were apparently the sound and tech people for the band. They worked together with blazing efficiency to roll out cables, test speakers, and to set up the unbelievably cool 'glass paper' screens. Two went up at opposite ends of the beer garden, along with speaker sets that any audiophile would envy. Bill wasn't the only one who drifted up to the screens, peering at them from a couple feet away like they were afraid they'd break them, even though they'd watched Gemma and Myles manhandle the things to get them into place.

In daylight, the big screens were basically transparent. At night, the darkness would provide enough of a backdrop to make anything displayed on them easily visible, although when one suddenly lit up in a test run,

Bill realized it was bright and high-res enough to be seen in everything but the very strongest sunlight. Laurie, standing at his side, whispered, "*Cool,*" like he was about eight, and Bill had to agree.

The other screens went up around the parking lot, twenty feet in the air on well-braced stands that were obviously designed to hold them. By then, Torbens were being recruited to help, although Bill stayed on the ground to watch. Myles slithered down the rigging to stand next to him for a minute, studying the screen above them critically. "Not bad. Crowd will love 'em."

"I love them," Bill said honestly. "What do you do when it's windy?"

The bassist smirked. "Mostly don't put 'em up. The bases are wide enough to give 'em stability, and they're hung to turn on an axis if the wind picks up that much. The only thing we can do at that point is take 'em down, but the key is that they're designed to *not* fall over and crush people in a stiff breeze. I checked the weather forecast. Wind's supposed to be low the next few days. Should be fine." He left Bill standing there, and went back to work.

They were set up and doing both video and audio tests on all the screens by about four in the afternoon, by which time Penny had somehow found crowd control barriers and was making Torbens arrange them in the parking lot. Bill, vaguely, said, "This might be illegal," and Penny, walking by, gave him a positively wolfish grin.

"I checked the town public gathering laws. There are house party limitations, but no block party or outdoors gathering size limits here. I'm betting there might be after this, but as of right now, this basically falls under the same laws as your Renaissance Faire thing, which means we could theoretically have about five thousand people show up before they could start throwing the book at us."

Bill gaped, and Penny grinned sharply again. "Don't worry, we're not expecting that many. But basically we can have as many people standing around a parking lot as we want, as long as there are clearly defined exit-ways and plenty of accessibility support. We've got two areas blockaded for people with mobility and other accessibility difficulties out here, and a space set aside up front inside."

"Wow. You're good at this, aren't you?"

"Baby, I'm *great*." Penny strode off again, leaving Bill to stare after her for a moment. She was incredibly fierce and he wouldn't have been surprised to get a shifter scent off her, but she seemed to just be a really strong-willed person. It was almost too bad. She'd make a great predator shifter.

His bear sniffed. *Doesn't smell like a threat.*

A predator and a threat aren't necessarily the same thing. Bill thought of house cats chasing black bears up trees, and grinned.

His bear sniffed again, with great offense this time. *Nothing* **attacks** *bears*, it said. *Not first. A bear is wise to retreat from something that attacks unprovoked.*

"You know what, I've watched angry cats going at veterinarians, and you're right. Nobody wants to fight a cat. Not even a bear." He went back into the pub, where half a dozen cousins and brothers were standing around, heads lowered together as they gossiped. Bill lumbered up and Ashley made room for him, elbowing Jon to the side, and all of them looked at Bill like they expected some kind of profound statement. "Don't ask me," he told them at large. "I have no idea what I've gotten us into here."

"I looked at the ticket sales," Jon said, "and then I called three people who were supposed to have the weekend off and offered them overtime to come work tonight and tomorrow. That's what you've gotten us into."

"Really? Thanks for doing that."

"Ashley made me."

Bill dropped his chin to his chest and chuckled. "Of course she did. Thanks, Ash."

"That redhead, Penny," Ashley said, sounding a bit smitten. "She went and laid out a plan for reducing crowding at the actual bar. She's got somebody picking up thingies. You know. Like in airport security lines. To cordon off the bar and have entrance and exit points. I've never seen anybody so organized." She *definitely* sounded smitten, and Bill couldn't help grinning.

"And she's a drummer in a rock and roll band. You should ask her out."

"Right. Because she has time to date when she's organizing a sell-out concert. There are forty people out there in high-vis vests, Bill. They're volunteer security to direct traffic and do crowd control. She's got them in a chat group so they can communicate during the concert. What is going *on* here? I don't mean any offense to Gwendolyn Brooker, but I don't think they'd be beating down the doors to see her and her jazz quartet tonight, and with this woman..." Ashley gestured broadly at the band's setup, the parking lot, the whole of it all. "It's like a flash mob concert. Who the hell *is* she?"

Emma Hart, Bill thought, but that really wasn't the answer, and he knew it. "She's Gwen Booker," he responded with a smile. "I talked to Mike Piccolo over at the Harlequin for a while last night and he said she'd walked away from a studio deal when she was young and was going it on her own. It just turns out that she and her band are really good at 'on their own,' I guess."

"I can't imagine what they'd do with a label," his cousin Luke said. "If they're doing this with five of them and a bunch of volunteers, they'd be selling out stadiums with a dedicated team."

"That's what Mike said. How are Mom and Dad taking it?" Bill raised his head, looking for his parents, who were nowhere to be found.

"They went out for an early dinner to 'get out of the young peoples' way,'" Laurie said. "They said they'd be back for the concert. Concert?"

"I think at this point it's a full-on concert, yeah," Bill said. "I'm beginning to think we should have sold gold-circle tickets for the inside and cheap seats for outdoors."

"Well, now you know for next year," Jon said brightly. Bill stared at him, and he said, "*What?* Don't tell me you're not booking her again next year! I mean, she's gonna be—" He broke off, obviously remembering

Bill hadn't told anybody else that Gwen was his mate, yet, and after a moment of flailing, redirected to, "— crazy popular, so why not take advantage of it?"

"Yeah, I think we've got a lot of things to talk about before that," Bill said. "But look, people are starting to show up already to make sure they get the good seats, so let's...woo." He exhaled. "Let's reserve some of them, all right? We've got a lot of long-time customers who bought tickets early for what was supposed to be Gwendolyn Brooker, so if they want premium seating for the Sixty Pix, they deserve that. How many people *did* cancel?"

"About forty percent of the tickets across tonight and tomorrow. But we resold them all, and then some," Jon said. "And it wasn't sold out for Ms Brooker anyway, so if we reserve maybe half the seats and tables...?"

Bill nodded. "Yeah. That sounds good. And Mike Piccolo wanted a good seat, so we need to save one for him, too. Thanks, Jon."

"No problem, bro." Jon broke away from the group and headed for the office, where Bill assumed he'd be printing out *reserved* signs. The others drifted apart, leaving Bill to stand in the middle of the pub, watching it begin to fill up hours before the show was meant to start. The clientele was completely different from their usual: younger, and much, *much* louder. They were also ordering food and beer like it was the start of a long night of partying, and, watching them go up to the bar, it was clear that very few, if any, of the people who had arrived so far were using the free beer pass Gwen had suggested. That was great for the bottom line, although Bill also hoped the people who'd bought early tickets *would* come, and that they wouldn't be disappointed with the show.

"You can't make everybody happy, cuz," Ashley murmured as she walked by.

"Am I that obvious?" he muttered after her.

Ashley stopped and came back to him. "You look like a man who's been given a million dollars and a kick in the gut at the same time. Look, Bill, the jazz thing worked for the pub for a long time, but a lot of that crowd have turned into people who are babysitting their grandkids on Friday or Saturday nights so *their* kids can get out on a date. I know the jazz festival is still huge here, but people haven't been turning up for the unofficial opening weekend here at the pub for a while, right? I think it's great that we're doing something different, even if you didn't quite mean to. Except I think subconsciously you did."

"Jon said something like that, too. I didn't think anybody else had noticed about the numbers falling off. I'm not doing such a great job here, Ash."

"Don't be ridiculous. You've taken on a job two people used to do and you're beating yourself up for not being able to do it all by yourself as well as they did. I tell you what, if this place was mine to run I'd really shake things up."

Bill, taken aback, said, "Seriously? Is that something you've thought about?"

"Oh my God, yeah, obviously. I love this place. I've always envied that it belonged to your parents and not mine. I'd have kicked my folks out ten years ago. Well. Okay, I was like seventeen ten years ago, but you know what I mean. Yeah, I'd love to manage this place," Ashley said wistfully.

"Why didn't you ever *mention* that?"

Her eyebrows shot up. "Because it *is* your parents' place, not mine, and you never ask for any help!"

Bill opened his mouth and shut it again as a cold ball of dismay sank all the way from his throat down through his stomach. "I ask Jon and Laurie…"

"No, you don't. Not the way you think you do. You've never sat them down and said, this is too much, I need you guys to pick up these specific tasks going forward. Have you." The last two words weren't a question at all. They *were* a challenge, and Bill flinched almost guiltily.

"I shouldn't have to! They're adults, they can see what's going on around them."

"They see their competent, responsible older brother handling it all, Bill. You ask them to do this or that, but they don't see it as an ongoing job, just something you can't do in the moment. And then you get really frustrated, and I get that. But they see this place as yours, not theirs, and they don't want to step on your toes."

"And you…?"

Ashley sighed. "I'm a woman, Bill. I want you to look up a thing online, a comic strip about mental load. Right now you're carrying a lot of mental load, but women end up doing it a lot, like a *lot* a lot, so maybe I can see it easier when you're doing it."

He stared at her a few seconds, then nodded. "Okay. I'll look it up. But, Ash, if you want to talk about managing the pub...this weekend probably isn't any good, but maybe after this craziness is all over?"

She smiled up at him. "Yeah, not now, but yeah, I'd really like that. Right *now*," she said, her smile growing, "you should go grab Gwen and take her and maybe the rest of the band over to the diner for something to eat in comparative peace and quiet before the show."

CHAPTER 21

Magically, just at the moment Gwen's energy was starting to flag post-setup, pre-show, Bill appeared at the little backstage area, said, "Let me take you all out to dinner. I think you're going to need something in your stomachs before the crowd demands your souls, because I'm pretty sure that's what's going to happen tonight," and shooed them all out a staff door to walk down the block toward a diner. None of them ate a lot—they rarely did before a show—but getting out of the venue and getting some fresh air and a little time to unwind was good for all of them. Tempers that had been fraying and tensions that were rising were restored, and by the time the band bounced back in the staff door half an hour before showtime, everyone was excited to get on stage.

Gwen hung back a moment, smiling up at Bill. "Thank you. That was just what we needed."

"Honestly, I should be taking you out for steak and

seafood or something. I can't believe how much of a crowd you've brought in."

"Oh, this whole mess was like handing candy to a baby for Penny. She thrives in an emergency, and she's incredible at rallying the troops. I'll see you after the show, all right?"

"Assuming I can make my way through your throngs of screaming fans, definitely."

Gwen laughed and, on impulse, stood on her toes to kiss the big man's cheek. He turned pink, and she made her way to the backstage area with the rest of the band, all of whom were now looking at her like Penny had done earlier. Gemma, in the tone of a band member who had seen far too many bad decisions on the part of its lead singer, said, "It's like that, is it?"

"Maybe." Gwen dimpled. "He's nice, anyway."

"Nice is good," Gemma opined, then lifted her chin at the stage. "We doing the new stuff for the encore or you wanna mix it it up in the main set?"

"Keep 'em here," Myles said. "Do it last except for *Midnight Kiss*."

"I am *not* playing until midnight," Sandy said automatically, and Myles gave her a lazy grin. They'd been making the same joke about the song name as long as they'd both been in the band, and it made Gwen smile every time.

"Someday I'm gonna make us do a ballad version of that song," Penny said, completing the ritual, and then they were on, walking out onto the little pub stage to a crowd that lifted its voice in a cheer.

Myles and Gemma had set up small screens at the

foot of the stage so they could see the camera work, which it turned out Bill's younger brother Laurie was a certified genius at, and one of the cousins—the pretty boy, Gwen couldn't remember his name—knew how to run a lights and sound board. So when Gwen yelled out, "Hello Renaissance!" a gorgeous drone shot of the town came up, then zoomed in on live outside footage of the pub, where there were a genuinely flattering number of people gathered, yelling their heads off, in the parking lot. "*HELLO, THUNDER BEAR!*"

The crowd raised the roof with their cheers that time, and the next forty minutes blurred into music and joy. From time to time a cue would come up on the screens and Gwen would yell something like, "Do I have *Denver* representing?" and road trip pictures—whether from actual drives, or selfies at the airport or flying into Renaissance—would come up on all the screens, featuring people who'd labeled themselves as #SixtyPix #RoadTrip #Denver #ShowTheWorld on their socials. Somebody outdoors was paying a lot of attention, and when the fans from Edmonton showed up late, a text came in on Gwen's little screen and the car full of Canadians climbed out to the whole crowd chanting, "ED-MON-TON! ED-MON-TON!" before dissolving into laughter and cheers. The Canadians clapped their hands over their faces, teary-eyed with smiles, and waved wildly at the screens as Gwen pointed at them through it.

There wasn't a better feeling in the world. They took a minute break, the whole band beaming at each other and slugging down bottles of water, then they were back on stage to play again, and then a third set before the noise ordinance hours started to threaten and they had to promise this was the last song, *honest.* Nobody even pretended to believe them, the shouts for an encore starting before they'd even left the stage.

After a minute, in the midst of the shouting, and to Gwen's jaw-dropped astonishment, they heard the chorus of one of the new songs, *Not Again,* that she'd played the night before being sung. The first lines were a little uncertain, but by the second half of the chorus an unbelievable number of people were singing with confidence, and when they hit the end, they rolled around to the beginning again. Penny whispered, "Holy shit," and even Myles, who took everything in stride, was round-eyed.

"Guys, I think we got a hit on our hands," he whispered. "Maybe we go out with that one, huh?"

"Yeaaaaaaaah," Sandy breathed. "Look, hey, how about I go out if they start again, and join in, and then the rest of you guys come in?"

Eager nods went around the band. Sandy grabbed a mic, waiting, and split a huge grin when the crowd started in on the chorus a third time. She came in on the second word, and by the fifth, before she'd even gotten on stage, the audience realized what was going on and their song broke into screams that made Sandy's eyes brighten with tears. She walked out, mic at her mouth, encouraging the crowd to come back in with her as she sang through a massive smile. Gwen watched, beaming, as Sandy fitted the mic into a stand and swung her guitar into place. She leaned into the microphone to sing as she came in with the guitar, and at the end of the chorus, murmured, "Now we're gonna bring it all back around to the beginning, yeah?" to a crowd absolutely losing its mind with anticipation.

Penny scurried out to the drums, making the audience cheer even more loudly, and Gemma gave Gwen a slow grin. "You're great at sharing the spotlight, G, but I think this time you're gonna have to stand in it. Let Sandy do the first verse. They'll lose their fuckin' minds when you come in on the chorus. C'mon, Myles." They went out together, waving and laughing as they took their places and Gemma brushed by Sandy to tell her the game plan.

She sounded so good Gwen almost didn't want to take the stage from her, but as Sandy reached the end of the verse, she pointed dramatically offstage at Gwen. Another shout rocked the rafters, and Gwen, shaking her head and smiling, brought the mic to her mouth and began to sing with her band as she walked on stage.

Not just with her band, but with the audience. They *knew* this song, a song she'd only played in public once, a day earlier. It was absolutely incredible, like flying, like dancing in the air, like she never, ever had to come back down to earth again. The whole band actually paused to take a bow at the end of the new song, before glancing at each other and slamming into the next one off the upcoming album. The one after that was a ballad, and then they ended on *Midnight Kiss*, an absolute banger Gwen had written about her love of fairy tales and happy endings.

Into the cheers and pleas for more encores at the end of it, she wrapped her fingers around the mic and said, "I swear we'd rather do nothing else but stay here all night and play for you until dawn, but somebody is actually going to come arrest us if we don't cut the noise now, so *thank you Renaissance*! We'll see you again tomorrow night!"

The band got together, took a bow, and went off stage, waving and blowing kisses until they hit the darkened backstage area and, almost as one, collapsed to the floor. Penny kicked her feet in the air, shrieking gleefully under the sounds of people still calling out for *one! more! song!* "The new album is going to blow up the charts, guys. Did you *hear* them? We might have to cut the set list short tomorrow and do all the new songs so far."

"Nah." Myles was sprawled across a remarkable amount of floor. "They can have *Not Again* if they come in singing the chorus like that again tomorrow, but otherwise stick with two new ones and that's it. The hype will be in getting to see us do them again officially for the first time."

"I thought Penny was supposed to be the marketing genius, not you," Sandy said happily. "Are we going outside to sign stuff?"

"*I* am waiting for the casuals to give up on us and leave," Gemma announced. "The die-hards will wait. Although I hope those girls from Calgary are—"

Everybody else shouted "*Edmonton!*" and Gemma cackled, making Gwen realize she'd done it on purpose. "The Canadians. I hope the Canadians stick it out, 'cause that's a hell of a drive."

Gwen's phone, in her back pocket, buzzed. She yelped and twitched to the side, taking it out, because a buzz stuck between her butt and a hard floor was surprisingly vibratey, and flicked to the incoming message. "Oh, uh, huh, wow, okay. Bill is asking if he can bring Mike Piccolo back to say hi. He's the guy who runs the Harlequin, the club I played at last night."

"Oh sure," Penny said without missing a beat. "Just don't expect me to get off the floor. It's nice and cool and I'm made at least ninety-eight percent of sweat right now."

"Guys?" Gwen asked. The rest of them made assenting noises, although like Penny, none of them seemed to have the slightest inclination to get up. They would soon, because the after-show adrenaline high was still coursing through them all and they'd want to go out and talk to the fans, but for the moment, lying on the floor recuperating was something of a Sixty Pix tradition. She texted Bill back with *Sure*, and a minute later he and Mike Piccolo came around the back of the stage. "Wow," she said to Bill, "you look *very* tall from down here."

He looked like a movable mountain, in fact, although she'd never imagined a mountain grinning like he was. The expression was half thrilled and half bewildered, which made sense, since there were five full-grown adults lying on the floor in his pub, and not even one of them was drunk. "Hi," he said from way up there. "That was incredible. Are you guys okay?"

Myles gave his traditional laconic thumbs-up, then let his arm flop back down to the floor. Mr Piccolo, who still looked like an 80s music producer even from this unusual angle, looked around at the band with laughter in his eyes. "Is this a modern musical act bonding ritual?"

Without discussing it, they all fumbled for each other's hands and lifted them, making a very lopsided circle of trust. *Or something,* Gwen thought with a smile. "It kind of is, yeah. Mr Piccolo—Mike—this is the Sixty Pix. Penny," she waved the hand that held Penny's in the air, "Gemma," with a wave of her other hand, holding Gemma's, "Myles, and Sandy." They each wagged their hands in the air, demonstrating which was which while Piccolo chuckled.

Then he crouched, putting himself a bit more on their level, which Gwen thought was a kind of nice gesture. She pushed up on her elbows to see him better, and so did everybody else, curiosity obvious in their expressions. "You kids know you've got a hit album on your hands, don't you?"

The band exchanged glances, and it was Penny who said a cautious, "Yeah?" over Gemma's muttered, "Not kids."

Sandy kicked her, and Myles let go an undignified snort of laughter. Mike Piccolo, who *was,* to be fair, literally old enough to be Gwen's father, and she was the oldest member of the band, looked like he was trying not to laugh the same way Myles had. "I know you've gone it alone, without a producer or a label, and I respect your reasons for that. But if you'd like to consider releasing the new album with a label's support, I'd like to ask you to keep Harlequin Renaissance Records in mind." He offered Gwen an old-fashioned print business card, nodded at the whole group of them, and rose to shake Bill's hand and then head out.

A little silence fell over the band, which mostly meant they lay there listening to the still-loud, happy crowd in the pub before Sandy said, "That was the least hard-sell producer I've ever met."

"Lemme see the card." Penny took it out of Gwen's hand. "Nice design. Good card stock."

Both were true, and it might be trite, but paying attention to small things like good design or card stock could really make a difference in how seriously a company could be taken. Gwen's heart still hammered, not in a good way, at the idea of that much potential *publicity*. She'd spent almost fifteen years going it the hard way to avoid that kind of thing.

Myles, phone lifted over his face, said, "Their website says Harlequin Renaissance Records has been putting out about three albums a year for the past thirty years or so. Whoozis there, Piccolo, he used to work for some really big labels before that, but— reading between the lines, here—he got disillusioned with the money-grubbing executives sucking up all the profit while the recording artists themselves ended up busting their balls to make rent. He retired, didn't like that either, and started HRR. He actually..." Myles trailed off, then cleared his throat. "He's got some bands whose names we know, guys. People I thought were full indie like us who have gotten national air play."

Gwen felt everyone's gazes shift from Myles to her, and took a breath to steady herself before saying, "Then maybe we'll have to talk about it. Talk to some of those bands and see what they think about working with him."

Another silence fell as the others exchanged looks and, with their gazes, pinned Penny as the spokesman. "G, you know we're okay with the way we're going, right? You don't have to, you know, risk everything for us."

"I'm one of five here, guys. It'd be pretty lousy of me to throw up a big roadblock on your careers because I've got issues."

Penny got to her feet, signaling to everybody else that they might as well get up, too, and offered Gwen a hand so she could grin at her. "G, baby, you've got *subscriptions*. Thank you," she said, although not to Gwen: she turned to Bill, who was standing awkwardly at the very edge of the stage shadows, trying to be present while also not being in the way. "Thanks for the intro, and for knowing to text Gwen to ask if it was cool before you did. Me and the rest of the band are gonna go out to meet the crowd. We'll try to winnow it down to the road-trippers before you come out, G. We'll text when it's safe. C'mon, losers," she said to the rest of the band, and a moment later, Gwen was alone in the dark with Bill Torben.

CHAPTER 22

"Is she always that subtle?" Bill asked as Penny disappeared with the other three band members.

Gwen laughed. "That was pretty subtle for her, actually. She didn't actually say anything like 'Gwen and Billy sittin' in a tree, k-i-s-s-i-n-g,' which I promise has been done in the past." She made her way to where he was at the edge of the stage, just in the shadows where the crowd couldn't see either of them, and sat.

Bill sat beside her and gave into the impulse to put his arm around her shoulders. To his relief and joy, she leaned against him immediately, exhaling into relaxation that turned to another laugh when he said, "Nobody's called me 'Billy' since I broke five feet at age nine."

"Jeez, really? That seems tall for that age. Maybe not for your family," Gwen added. "But still. Tall."

"It is. Not 'this kid has no choice but to be a pro basketball player' tall, but about half a foot taller than average. I outgrew my mom when I was twelve, and she's *tall*. Five ten. Also the shortest in our immediate family, but still tall!"

"I noticed. I'm a shrimp compared to the Torbens. I'm going to have to take up wearing four inch platform heels."

Bill, imagining her in those torn-up jeans and leather jackets in those kinds of heels, swallowed on a suddenly dry throat. "That'd put you right about six feet, wouldn't it? That would be...tall." *Tall* was not really what he was thinking of. *Hot* started to cover it, but a number of much more intriguing images involving her in short skirts and those heels were much closer to the mark. He wondered if she might have some leather bras to match those jackets, and then wondered who the hell he was. He'd never imagined anybody in leather bras before.

"Yeah, like, I'm about five eight, I'm not short, it's just you guys are all *tall*. It was a good show," she added in a complete change of subject, and with just the faintest hint of a question in her voice.

"A good show," Bill echoed disbelievingly. "Gwen, we sold just under five hundred tickets and there were people in the street that I'm sure didn't buy them. You guys brought the house down. I don't know why—I mean, I do, but—you should be selling out stadiums."

She leaned against him a little harder, turning her face against his shoulder, and when she spoke, her voice was a bit muffled. "I think we're on the cusp of something here," she admitted. "This is—tonight, this was something new. The way people showed up for us.

Um." She breathed deep, and exhaled even more deeply. "The Pix, we started by playing dives. Hell, we still play a lot of them. But, you know, forty, fifty people tops. Maybe a couple hundred if it was a popular bar, but that was more about the venue than *us*. The past few years, we've been pulling our own crowd, and, like, I know that. Two, three hundred people, mostly at places that don't hold a lot more than that so it feels like we're doing good, you know?"

Bill made a sound and Gwen shook her head, muffling a chuckle against his shoulder. "No, I know, we are good, but *doing* good in this industry is different. And I kinda know if we booked a venue that would hold five hundred, we've kind of reached a place where we'd be filling it. But I'd expect that to be with several months' notice, you know? People having time to find out about it, arrange to be there, all that. But this…they just showed up." She laughed again, the sound incredulous this time. "Five hundred people *just showed up* with barely a day's notice. And there's gonna be a new, maybe different, crowd tomorrow night."

"So." Bill turned his head to press his mouth against her hair. "On a scale of one to ten, how terrified are you?"

"I'm at about seventeen." Gwen fell silent a long time, and he thought he felt her shivering under his arm. "It's not just that if we lean into this moment everybody who doesn't know is going to realize I used to be Emma Hart. Although I don't think the band really gets how much that's going to be a thing, so it *is* that. But even more, it's…I've been successful," she said slowly. "Nobody tells you how scary it can be. How much you get judged and weighed and how much you judge yourself. How afraid you are that whatever you've done, you're never going to live up to it. That you can't repeat it. That you don't even know why it happened in the first place, even if you're good at what you do. So the truth is I'm really scared of succeeding. And that sounds *stupid*. People talk about fear of failure, of not trying things because what if you fail, but if you try something and succeed, then you're in completely new territory that you have no idea how to navigate, and that's *also* terrifying."

Bill, cautiously, said, "Especially when somebody took advantage of you the last time you succeeded?"

"Heh. Yeah, probably. Yeah." Gwen nodded. "That, and last time it was all really somebody else's doing. I was a kid. I was the talent, but I wasn't the driving force, right? Adults—my dad, showrunners, producers, whatever—were making most of the big decisions and I didn't even get that I could say no if I wanted to. And I'm not sure I really could have, because Dad would have…" She shrugged. "Pressured me. Told me how it was my Mom's dream, how every kid dreamed of this, how I'd be disappointing my audience. Things I felt like I couldn't refuse."

"It's just as well he disappeared," Bill said, trying to keep his voice light when he felt the words in his soul. "I'd be tempted to knock him into next week if he was around."

"You can get in line," Gwen said dryly. She hesitated.

"Do you think I'm nuts? For being scared that we're maybe on the verge of a breakout success?"

"No. No, not at all. Partly because you actually do have experience in being, what, successful? Famous? In ways the rest of us are probably never going to. But also because you're right. I don't think I ever really thought about it, but everybody kind of assumes success is its own reward, don't they? I never thought about as being scary all by itself, but what you said about being out there in new territory, dealing with you don't even know what because you've never been there before, that makes a lot of sense. I wonder." He breathed a short little laugh. "I wonder if that's part of why I haven't tried changing anything around here."

"Hah!" Gwen looked up at him, her dark-rimmed eyes clear and gorgeous in the dim light. "Look at us, birds of a feather."

"Bears," Bill said with a chuckle. "Bears of a fur."

"You've got a real thing about bears, big man. What's that about?"

Now! his bear said eagerly. *This is the right time! Tell her now!*

The bear was absolutely right. It *felt* right, emotionally. This was the moment he'd been waiting for.

The problem was that Gwen was very, very unlikely to believe him unless he shifted into a grizzly, and doing that backstage in a pub with hundreds of people a few feet away, and a back door that might open without warning at any moment, was *obviously* a bad idea. Bill put his forehead against Gwen's and sighed.

"My family likes them. Has an affinity for them, you might say."

"Because you're all huge?" Gwen grinned, almost against his mouth. "Yeah, I can see that."

"Well—" He was just about to give in and explain—to *show* her—when the back door did, in fact, sweep open and Penny threw herself in, then mashed the door shut again. Bill's shoulders collapsed in resignation as Penny stared, wild-eyed and dramatic, at Gwen.

"They are literally chanting your name," she informed Gwen. "Hundreds of them. I do not think this crowd is going to thin out until after you've put in an appearance. I *did* get some of the security crew to herd the Canadians off to one side so they can meet us later, but G, we are at the start of a moment. A movement. I completely get your reservations, and also, I will totally kill you if you blow this for the rest of us."

Bill bristled a little, prepared to defend Gwen's decisions, whatever they were, but to his surprise, she cackled and stood up. "Yeah, no, that's fair. Like I said, I'm one of five, it would really suck for me to bring everybody else down."

"You're not, you know." Penny was watching the singer with an intense gaze. "I mean, you are, yes, but some animals are more equal than others, even if you go to huge lengths to keep yourself out of the limelight except when we're actually on stage. The truth is you could walk away and have a solo career in a way none of the rest of us could, or you could decide to stay right here behind this door and make sure we never climb any higher than we are right now. And I *would* totally kill you, but I'd also get it."

Gwen made a face that looked like it came from the bottom of her soul. "You know I'd never go solo."

"Yes. But I also know you could."

The face Gwen made that time was more resigned than rejecting, and she walked over to give Penny a heavy hug. "Yeah. I could. And I could also not go out there right now and just let you guys enjoy the glory."

"But it's not what they want, and we know it," Penny said gently to the lead singer. "They got their time with us. Now they want to see the main event."

"I'll come with you, if you want," Bill offered quietly. "You said I made good security."

"'You *are* the brute squad,'" Penny said to him, and Gwen laughed, then put a hand out toward Bill momentarily, accepting his offer with the gesture.

"That would be great, yeah. For the record, I'd be okay without the brute squad, but it'd be nice to have it. All right." She gave Penny a nervous grin. "Let's go blow the roof off this thing, I guess."

"Damn straight." Penny grabbed her hand and pulled the door open to a roar that nearly knocked Bill backward. Even she said, "Oh my God," under her breath, and then the two band members were out in the beer garden, pulled into a security line of people guiding them down toward the crowd.

Bill fell in right behind them, abruptly aware of his own size in a way he usually wasn't. The women looked *small* in front of him, and it was clear that the people clustered around the cordons just off the beer garden all suddenly felt like maybe it wasn't *quite* as important as they'd imagined to be the first ones to touch, or get pictures with, the band's star. One of the security guys—not someone he knew, but a shifter from the sense of him—gave Bill a brief, approving nod that gave him an odd sense of satisfaction. The security dude couldn't possibly know Bill was there to protect his mate, but it felt like he'd been recognized as Doing His Job, and he liked it.

It was much, much more chaotic than the Harlequin had been the night before. For one thing, although there'd been a couple hundred people at that gig, only two dozen or so had hung around after the show. Tonight there were five times that number, some of them with the frenzied, glittering looks that Bill had seen in videos of Elvis, or the Beatles.

His bear rumbled. *Those people aren't safe for our mate.*

Most of them are, Bill disagreed, and honestly believed it. But it did make him remember that *fans* was short for *fanatics.* He'd never really been in the firing line of that kind of intensity before.

But Gwen had, he realized. He knew it: she'd told him. He just hadn't fully understood, not until right now, and he bet that this—a last-minute gig at the edge of the Rockies—wasn't anything compared to what she'd experienced as a kid in Hollywood.

The bear rumbled again. *These people aren't safe for **us**.*

That, unfortunately, could well be true. Shifters usually tried to stay out of the spotlight, and with good reason. But nothing external told the world Bill could turn into a giant grizzly, and he said, *Well, we're certainly not going to shift in front of them. It'll be fine,* with as much calm reassurance as he could. It was something he hadn't considered, though. Maybe it wasn't possible to safely build a relationship with a burgeoning rock star while living in a small shifter town.

He'd never really considered leaving Renaissance, before. Not until that moment. But as he watched Gwen laughing and bumping elbows and taking selfies with fans, signing things—including their faces—for them, he realized that whether *she* knew it or not, she was in her element. This was *her* fate, and he knew in his heart that she was ready to embrace it.

Which might mean his own fate was a future he'd never even dreamed of.

ill stayed with her right through the whole line, a large comforting presence who never once had to say anything, much less *do* anything to offer protection. Being there was enough. More than enough. They met the Canadians—a gorgeous pair of women who gotten married recently and were declaring the road trip an extension of their honeymoon—and had a few seconds with many of the other road-trippers, all of whom were almost incoherent with joy. Gwen felt that way herself, buzzing with excitement and remembering, for the first time in a long time, the *fun* parts of this kind of life.

It was late when the last fans finally drifted away. Late enough that the pub's kitchen would have closed down already, except Bill had gone back to ask them to stay open so the band could eat. By then they were all starving, but still giddy, half shouting at each other about the evening's successes. Bill went to man the grill himself, a big solid guy who obviously knew what he was doing, although when Gwen complimented him, he shook his head and smiled. "I'm okay in a kitchen. You should try my brother's place out in New York, though. They've turned it into a gourmet gastropub."

"Right," Gwen said, amused, "because New York is a very practical place to have lunch before the gig tomorrow. Or for our date next weekend."

His brown eyes genuinely lit up, as if he'd thought she would have forgotten their plans for the next weekend. "Maybe on the third date," he offered.

Gwen laughed out loud and raised her beer bottle to him. It was *great* beer—this one was called Thunder Blunder, and was apparently one of their most popular IPAs—and if she wanted to be hung over for the next gig, she'd have several. Instead she nursed the one, then accepted a second that she'd drunk most of before she realized she was supposed to drive back to the hotel. She swore about it rather philosophically, trying to figure out in her head how long it would take to walk before she got her phone out and checked the map app.

"I know at least two of the band haven't been drinking," Bill said, settling down at her side, "but I could drive you, if you wanted."

"Why Mr Torben," Gwen said rather hopefully, "you don't have ulterior motives, do you?" He looked so startled she couldn't help laughing again. "I guess not, then."

"No," he said sheepishly. "Not beyond thinking 'and that way I can come pick you up again in the morning, since your car will be here.'"

"Oh, so you *are* planning ahead. Good to know. Are we having breakfast together?"

"I'd love that. What time do you wake up after a gig?"

"I told you. About three in the afternoon. Oh, all right. I can manage eleven or so. Even ten, if I absolutely have to, but I'd better get to sleep soon if that's going to happen."

"Saturday morning brunches are a thing around here," Bill admitted. "Ten is a lot easier to get a seat at a restaurant than eleven or twelve is."

"We could order room service."

He blinked at her, then, catching her meaning, blushed again. Gwen put her beer bottle down and reached up to scruff his chin, fingers tangled in his short beard. "I don't know if you've always blushed easily or if it's just me—"

"It's *definitely* just you."

Her smile widened. "But I love it. Is that a yes?"

Bill groaned and leaned in to put his forehead against hers like he'd done earlier. It was so effortlessly intimate it made her sigh, a soft contented sound, and a feeling inside her to match. "I would love to," he said reluctantly. "But there's still some stuff I need to tell you, and I'd rather you were completely sober for it, honestly."

Gwen leaned back, examining him. His dark gaze was soft, but quite certain. "It's that bad? Or is it me? Because don't take this wrong, but men don't usually turn me down twice."

He groaned again, though this one had some

amusement in it. "No, I don't imagine they do, and I'm kind of kicking myself for doing it. It's not bad, and it's definitely not you, but I think once I've explained you'll agree sober is better. Even if you're not actually drunk."

She squinted at him, more mock-suspicious than really suspicious. "This isn't some kind of weird over-protective male thing, is it? Because that crap doesn't cut it with me."

"I'm not gonna say I'm not enjoying being the huge security guy at your back, but no, it's not like that. I promise. So can I drive you home, or should I let you go with your band?"

Gwen wrinkled her nose, then sighed. "I think I should go home with the band, because otherwise I'll try to persuade you to make bad choices. I like you," she added, suddenly feeling like it might not be obvious. "And I tend to be a go-after-what-I-like kind of person."

"I don't think I've ever met anyone like you," Bill murmured. "And I'm weak in the face of beautiful, persuasive women, so, all right. I'll see you in the morning for breakfast?"

"Perfect," Gwen said a bit wistfully. Getting laid after a great show would have been the ideal way to end the night. On the other hand, there was something a bit charming about Bill's insistence on talking about things first, whatever those things might be. "I, oh. I was about to give you my keys so you could just drive the Impala over in the morning, but you're nine feet tall and you'd have to move my seat back. You'll just have to bring me here after breakfast. Or, oh, wait! Do you hike?"

"I like to run around in the woods," Bill said in a funny tone.

Gwen beamed. "If we've got time after breakfast, maybe we can go for a little hill walk. It's good for me to get out of my head and move around some before a show. Especially one..." She trailed off, and Bill leaned in to give her a sudden, soft, unexpected kiss that made warmth spill through her whole body.

"Especially one that might be leading up to making some big life decisions. I'll bring canteens and some trail snacks and we'll hit my favorite trail after breakfast."

She felt her smile go as funny as his tone had been. "Are you for real, Bill Torben? Out here being the perfect guy?"

He ducked his head and glanced up again, expression oddly shy. "Would it be too corny if I said I hoped I *was* the perfect guy for you?"

"No." She'd only known the man a day and a half, but Gwen felt more confident of that answer than she had of anything in her entire life. "No, I think that would be just about right. I don't know why, because that seems ridiculous, but there you have it."

"Maybe we'll figure it out tomorrow."

❧

BREAKFAST WAS GOOD; the hike up into the lower part of the mountains was better, with the autumn leaves just starting to go gold, and a brisker crispness to the air than was obvious in the town, only a few hundred feet lower. Bill brought Gwen up to a lookout, where she collapsed into a wooden bench slightly more dramatically than was necessary. But only slightly. A little breathlessly, she said, "I should hike more," and Bill shook his head, smiling.

"I've just watched you bounce around on stage for over two hours, two nights in a row. Your cardio must be amazing."

"Oh, it is, but only for flat surfaces. I don't do hills. You, on the other hand, are not only the size of a mountain, but can apparently just, like, waltz up them effortlessly."

"I have an advantage there." Bill sounded nervous enough that Gwen sat up from her dramatic collapse to smile at him.

"Is it that you live at the base of a mountain range and can go for a hike through the woods any time you want to?"

"No. Although, yes, that too, but…no. There's some-thing I need to tell you about myself that will clarify it. Maybe. I think. Either that or you're going to run away screaming."

Gwen's eyebrows rose. "Wow. That's. Wow. I don't think I've ever had a guy say that to me before, and I've heard a lot of lines. For the record I'm not sure that's a great one."

Bill passed a hand through his hair, messing up his pompadour. "No, I guess it isn't. It's just, I said last night it was something to talk about and you should be sober?"

"Yeah, and before that you wanted to tell me something and I assumed it was 'hey, I know you used to be Emma Hart and I've been hot for you since I was a teen,' which was about as wrong as I could be, so I think I won't try guessing again. What's up?"

"This is. Woo. I never did this before—"

Gwen's jaw fell open. "You're a virgin?"

"What? No! What? *No!*" Whatever was bothering Bill, the question surprised him so much that he looked indignant. "I mean, I hope it wouldn't bother you if I was, but no! It's much weirder than that!"

"Being an adult virgin isn't that weird!"

"That's my point! No, I'm not a virgin, I'm a bear!"

Gwen opened her mouth to—she didn't know what. Laugh, say *what?* herself, maybe make a comment about the thing he seemed to have about bears—and while she was waiting to find out how she was about to respond, Bill Torben changed into a bear.

It was the most incredible, peculiar thing she'd ever seen. He shivered, sort of, or twisted, or—*something*, she couldn't quite describe it—and changed, in the space of a heartbeat, from a big tall thick man to a perfectly enormous grizzly bear. Like, a truly truly *huge* bear, not that Gwen had any real sense of how big grizzlies were, not up close and personal, but this one was obviously a magnificent specimen. He was on all fours, which didn't make much sense because he'd been standing on two legs when he changed, but on the other hand Gwen didn't know why she was concerned about minor things like that when a *man* had just *turned into a bear* in front of her.

Gwen, in what she thought was a very moderate, calm, and reasonable response, said, "Holy fucking shitballs."

The bear laughed. It was obviously a laugh. How she knew it was a laugh and not a threatening huff, Gwen didn't know, but it was definitely a laugh. Then he changed back into Bill, who was standing on his own two feet instead of on all fours like would make sense, and was smiling like he'd just ended a laugh. Gwen said, "Holy fucking shitballs," again, and discovered she had somehow climbed over and behind the bench she'd been sitting on. She petted it nervously a couple of times, then edged back around to the front, although she stood with the back of her knees pressed against the seat rather than coming any closer to Bill quite yet.

She wasn't exactly scared, she didn't think. Flabbergasted. Mostly her mind was filled with variations on 'holy fucking shitballs,' and she thought it might take a minute to get past that. When she did, it was with a squeaked, "Why weren't you on your feet? Your, uh, your back feet? When you, uh, when you did that, you were standing on your, on your human feet," and oh God that sounded insane, but Bill had a small, encouraging, hopeful smile while she bumbled her way through the question. "But then when you changed you were on all four feet, why weren't you on two feet. And why weren't you on your hands and knees when you changed back again?"

"I guess because I was thinking of myself as stand-ing, and humans stand on two feet and bears usually stand on four." He still sounded like a person. And looked like one.

Gwen's heart was beating so hard she thought it would probably crash out of her chest and fly away. "And you, um. Clothes?"

"Things I'm wearing shift with me unless I don't want them to, but I've never found a pair of jeans that will accommodate being stretched across a grizzly-sized ass. The Hulk," he said solemnly, "is really lucky with those purple shorts of his."

A brief, high-pitched laugh escaped Gwen, then turned into a series of real giggles as she sat abruptly, staring up at the big man. "An 'affinity' for bears, huh? Isn't that what you said? Your whole family is like this? Are you—are there—?"

"There are more shifters than you'd think, yes, but not that many of us in the grand scheme of things." Bill crouched, clearly making an effort to be smaller and less alarming, but Gwen didn't think she was alarmed anymore. Or even sure she had been. Just astonished.

"You're okay," she said. "I'm not scared. Just...holy fucking shit."

He grinned lopsidedly. "Yeah, I know."

"I am on the pill, you know," Gwen said vaguely. Bill's eyebrows shot up and she said, "I assume that's why you wanted to tell me before we had sex. Because I assume there must be some chance of, you know. Baby bears?"

Bill thumped back on his butt, looped his arms

around his knees, and laughed. "Ah. Right. No. I mean, yes, we don't breed a hundred percent true, but most shifter parents do end up with shifter kids. But I wasn't really thinking about unexpected pregnancies. I also have condoms," he added, almost as vaguely, then went red around the ears. "Hope springing eternal, and all that. No, I just...um. There's. Uh. More?"

"More. Than turning into a bear." Gwen held up a palm before he spoke. "Is it extremely, *extremely* important that I learn this 'more' right now?"

The big man held his breath a moment, looking as if he was seriously considering the question. "I don't think so," he said slowly. "It's all kind of tied together, but...no. Not if the whole shifter thing isn't a deal-breaker."

"I don't think it is. I mean, it's not. It's...I have so many questions." Gwen laughed. "*So* many questions. Like do you tell all your prospective partners you're a bear? You must be very selective if you do, because that can't be safe. But no, I'm good, I'm..." She stared at him a moment, then wet her lips. "Like, don't take this wrong, because I'm not into *bears*, per se, but...I mean, talk about meeting a guy in touch with his animal side. That's really..." She cleared her throat. "Really hot."

Bill's deep brown eyes went bright with a smile. "I have those condoms *with* me, just to be clear."

"I also have a recently-discovered yet long-held fantasy about getting fucked by a guy big enough to pin me up against a wall without being afraid I'd get dropped," Gwen said breathlessly. "But there aren't any walls around here."

"Who needs walls?" Bill rose in an incredibly smooth surge and strode to her in a couple of steps, lifting her off the bench, hands beneath her ass to wrap her legs around his waist. Gwen gave a startled squeak even as her entire body lit up with heat and need as his mouth found hers, although the kiss only lasted long enough for her core to turn molten before he broke off enough to laugh against her lips. "I didn't think this through. I should've gotten you naked *before* I picked you up, because now I don't want to put you down again."

For a couple frantic seconds Gwen tried to work out the physics of that before laughing in despair against his mouth in turn. "Nope, can't make it work. I can get to all of *your* important bits, but damn, I should've worn a skirt, big man."

He rumbled so deeply it ran through her bones, melting them before he kissed her again, long and deep and slow. She'd more or less forgotten her name by the time that kiss ended, and was trying to meld her body with his through two layers of denim and presumably some cotton underwear. Even through all of that he felt astonishing pressed against her center, a promise of complete satisfaction. She was just about to reluctantly get her feet back on the ground so she could yank her jeans off when laughter and voices came from farther down the trail, and they yelped against each other's mouths in dismay.

"Tonight," Bill breathed. "Wear a skirt for the show tonight, and afterward we'll pick this up right where we left off."

"I never wanted a performance to be over so bad in my life." Gwen was on the edge of throwing all caution to the wind, personally, but Bill, laughing again, put her on her feet, and bent to kiss her again just before a small crowd of hikers came into the lookout clearing.

"Me either," he promised her. "Me either."

CHAPTER 24

On second thought, Bill realized, they should have just turned right around and gone back to his house, or Gwen's hotel. It was only about one in the afternoon when the other hikers interrupted them, but for some damn reason, he thought *finishing the hike* was a better idea than cutting it short and taking the afternoon to themselves.

The funny thing was, Gwen apparently thought so too, because when they got up to the trail's summit, she suddenly blurted, "We're idiots. We could have gone back to the hotel," which made Bill laugh out loud, the sound bouncing around the rocks and trees.

"I was just thinking that. I guess I just got it in my head that we were going on a hike and the only way to finish that was to actually finish it. It was way shorter to go back than finish by going around."

She slid her hand, small and warm, into Bill's. "At least we're the same kind of idiot. And this has been nice. Not that going back to the hotel wouldn't have been, but..." She sighed. "For a woman who lives in Denver, a notoriously get-outside-and-do-stuff city, I don't really get outside all that much. I'm either at work or rehearsing. So this has probably been really good for me, even if," she lifted a knee up and down, making a face, "even if my butt and legs are wondering what the hell I'm doing. I haven't walked up this many hills in ages. And now we have to walk down them again!"

"Your job must be pretty flexible?" They started down the trail as it bent back toward the distant parking lot.

"More flexible than my butt, man. Ow. I'm not going to be able to bounce around on stage tonight." Gwen didn't sound like she meant a word of the complaints as she moved ahead of Bill on the trail. Her butt looked just fine from his vantage. Better than fine, in fact. She had a great round little ass that had fit into his hands wonderfully, and it was probably just as well he *hadn't* thought to depants her before picking her up, because those hikers showing up would have really gotten an eyeful in that case. She called, "It's a part-time job except if there's a crunch. They're a fulfillment business and mostly only need somebody to answer phones in the mornings, although it gets crazy around the holidays, obviously. So they're usually cool with me taking a long weekend most of the year, and sometimes I just have the office phone forwarded to mine for a few hours every day so I can work remotely anyway."

"An ideal job for a rock star," Bill called back as she skipped a little ahead. She was a dark streak in the golden leaves and soft autumn light, bouncing from one step to another like someone who spent a lot more time outdoors than she claimed she did. He felt unbelievably content just watching her, as if he could spend the rest of his life doing exactly that and think it was a life well lived.

That reminded him, suddenly and wonderfully, of his parents, and he found himself grinning like an idiot the whole rest of the way back to the truck. "Is the pub okay? You'll want your car."

"And a shower," Gwen agreed. "I didn't take one last night because I knew we were going hiking this morning. I'm surprised you can't smell me from halfway across the state." Her eyes widened. "*Can* you?"

"Only from a couple miles."

Gwen snapped her gaze around to him and he spread his hands. "Bears have great senses of smell. Humans aren't nearly as good, but shifters do mostly scent and hear better than true humans."

"Holy crap! Oh my God! I'll remember to stay showered!"

"You smell good," he assured her. "You smell great, in fact."

"Nope. Showering. Now, forever, always. Well, not now. But once we're back in town. And I would invite you to join me, but," she sighed, "exercise early in the day before a concert is good for me. Exercise late in the day is less good, but better than nothing. Both, however, would wipe me out."

"Oh, you think I'd exercise you?"

Gwen looked him up and down as they climbed

into his truck and dropped her voice into a purr. "Big man, I'm counting on it."

*She **likes** us,* his bear informed him with enthusiasm.

Bill groaned aloud, both agreeing with the bear and acknowledging Gwen's flirting. "Are you sure we can't go back to your hotel? Or my house?"

"I'm sure I'm trying to make good decisions for the show tonight," Gwen said, not very convincingly, though she followed it with a snort. "Penny would actually murder me if I showed up low-energy tonight."

"Okay, that seems pretty likely," Bill admitted. "She's fierce."

"She really is. We met at an audition for somebody else's band and she was like 'screw these guys, let's make an all-girl band of our own.' I didn't know she'd recognized me for two years. The woman can keep a secret."

"That's impressive. But, er, Myles?"

"Came with Gemma. Package deal. He's the only guy we've ever had in the lineup. I'd say he has big feminine energy, but it's not true. He *is* a tech genius, though, and the band is lucky to have him. Oh, my God." That was as they approached the pub, which actually had a crowd gathered, sitting on benches that had magically appeared in the parking lot, as far as Bill could tell. "That can't be for the show tonight. There must be a hundred of them already."

"I'm pretty sure it can be. Um, do you want to go in there? You might never get out again."

"I think I'd better not," Gwen said, wide-eyed. "Can you drive me to the hotel? I'll get a lift back over with

Penny before the show, but holy crap, Bill, what have we done?"

"I think you might have broken out," Bill said honestly. "The Sixty Pix have escaped containment. That's amazing, Gwen."

"I was not planning for this."

"Life is what happens when we're making plans, right?" Bill drove past the pub and stole a kiss when he dropped Gwen off outside the hotel. "I'll text you directions to the back parking lot where the staff park. I think you guys should come in that way tonight. I'm going to go back and start setting up security and..." He trailed off, thinking of the number of people already hanging out at the pub. "And see if I can call anybody else to help cover tonight. You know, I think you might have changed my life, Gwen."

"Seems fair." She paused in the truck door, smiling at him. "Because I think you've changed mine, too." She blew him a kiss, and was gone.

Bill watched where she'd gone for a moment, smiling and shaking his head. He *thought* she'd changed his life? No, he knew it. But fated mates was still a lot to drop into a casual conversation, and she was right. That part of the conversation could wait. She'd accepted him as a bear; the rest of it was working out the details.

He took the route back to the pub that he was going to send the band, and parked in the back lot. His parents' vehicle was there, along with a couple of the cousins' cars and more staff vehicles than he would have expected. He went inside to semi-organized chaos, and his cousin Ashley flagged him down. "Hey, cuz. I knew you had a date this morning, so when people started showing up I thought I'd take the bull by the horns and called in some reinforcements."

"I'm going to have to back-date your starting date and give you a raise and a promotion. How does 'Head Boss Manager of the World' sound as a job title?"

"I'll want business cards with that." Ashley grinned like she didn't believe Bill had meant it, and went off to order his younger brothers around, yelling, "Hey, your parents are in the event room!" to Bill over her shoulder.

"So I take it you don't need me in here right now," Bill said under his breath. He was definitely hiring her with a raise already built in, whether she believed him or not. He grabbed a root beer—the one non-alcoholic drink the brewery also made—and went to the event room, which could be used either for private events or spillover space if the rest of the pub filled up. They'd opened it the night before, and Bill knew they'd be opening it tonight, too.

For the moment, though, his parents were slouched comfortably in a couch in there together, drinking coffee and chatting. They both looked up as he came in, and his mother smiled fondly at him. "Hello, sweetheart. I'm so proud of you."

"Oh good. Thanks. Why?" Bill dropped into the couch across from them and put his root beer on the table, watching bubbles rise.

"For this transition," his mother said in surprise.

"We had no idea you were taking the pub this direction."

Bill blinked. "Um. Uh. What?"

"Oh, come on, sweetheart. We really believed it, you know. When you posted to the family chat and said you'd messed up the booking, we thought you were serious. And I'm not going to pretend I didn't panic. You don't make mistakes like that."

"I—"

"But you can't really believe us to expect you put crowds like this together literally overnight," his father went on, oblivious to Bill's faint protests. "I wish you'd felt comfortable letting us know you were going to try something new, but this has been a terrific effort, Bill. I know jazz and the Renaissance Jazz Festival were always your mother's and my thing, but I didn't realize rock was such a passion of yours. That young woman is a real star. How long have you been a fan of hers?"

Bill opened his mouth and shut it again.

"She certainly seems to like you, too." His mom's eyes sparkled. "It might not be fate, baby, but maybe you've found somebody worth your time?"

"It is fate, actually," Bill said with a stupid little grin.

Both his parents jolted upright, his mom visibly suppressing a squeal. "What? Really? *Really*, Bill?"

"Yeah." His smile grew, almost embarrassed. "I haven't told her yet. I did tell her—I showed her—my bear, which she, well, you know, there was a lot of swearing and staring, but that seems reasonable, right? I was going to tell her the rest of it but we got interrupted." By almost having sex. He was nearly forty, but he didn't feel the need to mention that to his parents.

"Oh my God! It's about time!" His mother clapped her hands together, and his dad gave her a fond, exasperated look.

"Heather. You can't rush fate."

"Yes, yes, I know, but it's still about time! Bill! Sit down and tell us everything!" His mother pointed imperiously at the couch he was already sitting on. Both he and his father laughed, and she *hmph*ed in mock insult.

"I don't know what to tell you, Mom. She blew in like a hurricane on Thursday and I just knew. I've been following her around making moon eyes ever since." He decided not to mention his absolute certainty that Gwen's arrival spelled disaster for the pub, because it seemed he'd been more wrong about that than anything in his entire life. "She played a publicity gig at the Harlequin on Thursday and Mike Piccolo—he says hi, by the way—said her band was on the verge of a breakout. I think he might be right. I think this might be the weekend that changes everything."

His parents were both beaming as they said, "That's *wonderful*," in chorus. A heartbeat later, though, his mother moved on to all the implications of that, things Bill had barely even let himself think about yet, and her face fell. "Oh. That's…complicated. I mean, what about the pub, Bill?"

"What *about* the pub?" his dad asked, baffled, then followed his mother's train of thought. "Oh. Oh, so she's going to be…traveling a lot? What does that mean for you, Bill? For the pub?"

"I literally haven't thought about it. I haven't had time. I…" Bill swallowed. "It might not mean anything. I don't know. I don't know at all."

"We can come back from Tucson for a while," his mom said dubiously. "But with this new direction you're taking things, it'll be a step backward to have us running the place again. This is your business now, Bill."

The impulse to just say *I don't want it* rose up in him so strongly Bill bit his tongue. It wasn't exactly true. He loved running the actual brewery. The *pub* was the part he found exhausting. After a long moment, hoping he could trust his voice, he managed to say, "Let me think about things a little, Mom. Dad. The past couple days have been a lot. The truth is I think I need someone else to manage the pub anyway."

Confusion filled his parents' eyes. Bill forged ahead, trying to speak clearly but also quickly enough that they couldn't interrupt and start to argue. "I was talking to Ashley earlier and she pointed out that I've been trying to do two jobs for the last five years. You two used to share the work I'm doing alone. I hadn't thought of it like that, and it…" To his horror, his throat tightened with the threat of tears. He cleared it and tried to continue. "It helped me understand some of why I've felt so overwhelmed. I don't want to disappoint either of you, but I can't keep doing two full time jobs."

"Baby," his mother said in astonishment. "I didn't, *we*

didn't know you were feeling this way. Why didn't you say something?"

His father exhaled heavily. "Because he didn't want to disappoint us, Heather. And to be fair," he said to Bill, "I never quite thought of it that way either. Your mother spent a lot of time raising you kids, but we only had the brewery when *you* were really little, and you were a big help with your brothers by the time we opened the pub. By the time the pub became a going concern, she was able to do most of the brewery management while I got the pub off the ground. I knew we were a partnership. I didn't think about how handing it over to you meant giving you two jobs to fill by yourself. I'm sorry, son."

"What about your brothers?" Bill's mother still sounded mystified. "They help out, don't they?"

Bill sighed. "They spend April through September doing ren faires, Mom. Sometimes March through October. They're great promotion for the brewery. Between their efforts and Steve out in New York we've expanded our customer base across half the country now. But..." He remembered how Ashley had phrased it, and echoed that: "They do what they're asked. They don't seem to see slack that needs to be picked up, much less *do* that."

His mother's mouth tightened. "That's inexcusable. I raised them to be more responsible than that."

"You raised our oldest son, Mr Responsibility, and our second-oldest, who left town to go have his own responsibilities instead of tending to the family's," his dad said wryly. "I suspect Bill's been picking up slack for his younger brothers for most of his life, Heather. Older siblings tend to. Which you know. And so do I."

Bill was grateful his father had said it so he didn't have to, and even more grateful that someone *noticed.* "It's fine," he said quietly. "I just can't keep doing it on my own, and if Jon and Laurie don't want to, I need to find someone else. It's not going to be Gwen," he said almost fiercely. "She's got an incredible career right at her fingertips and there's no way I'm going to ask her to give that up."

"And I think we need to consider the possibility that you'll go to support her," his father said just as quietly.

Bill's heart lurched. He hadn't really let himself think about that, either. His mother's jaw fell open, complex emotions dancing over her face as considered the idea. Then she inhaled. "I suppose we really might need to look at coming back from Tucson, then."

"I don't know, Mom. Ashley's out there taking over right now, running Jon and Laurie and everybody else like a pro. I've already offered her a job twice, but I don't think she believes me. Just...this is all really new. I need some time to think about things. Okay?"

"Of course." His father spoke again, then offered a smile very like Jon's crooked one. "I'm sorry you didn't tell us about this before, Bill, but I'm glad it's out in the open now. And I'm thrilled for you. Gwen is a hell of a woman."

Bill felt his smile go silly with joy. "A literal rock star. Completely out of my league."

"She most certainly is not!" his mother said indignantly. "A good, solid, reliable, kind man like you? Most rock stars should be so lucky!"

Bill laughed and stood so he could kiss his mom on the cheek. "Not that you're in any way biased."

"I'm not!" She looked even more indignant as both her husband and son laughed. "I'm not! I'm absolutely right! Aren't I, Pete?"

"You are," Bill's father agreed. "But that doesn't mean you're not biased."

"I am not!"

Bill, feeling lighter than he had in months, left his parents to their good-natured disagreement, and went to find his fated mate.

CHAPTER 25

Sneaking in the back way brought back memories for Gwen. Not necessarily good ones, although for the first time, she thought maybe they weren't entirely bad, either. The rest of the band were exchanging slightly hysterical glances as they scurried from the back parking lot into the pub's kitchen, and from there, through the staff hall to Bill's office. Gwen still had a key, and let them all in, though there weren't enough chairs and she ended up sitting on the floor against the filing cabinets while the others nabbed what chairs there were, and, in Penny's case, sat on the desk.

Penny was the one who asked: "Is it always like that?" There were easily three hundred people already at the pub, most of them in the parking lot, and they were making a lot of noise, even this early in the evening.

Gwen thumped her head against the cabinets and smiled, then shook her head. "No. For bigger stuff you end up coming in from a distant entrance most of the fans don't even know about. It's less sneaky, or it feels less sneaky, because you can't hear them, or see them. It's safer. Less overwhelming. Under the right circumstances, though, going in through the crowd is…it's fun, in a way. You really get hyped up for the show."

Myles had thrown his long legs over the arm of the chair he'd taken. "I don't think I've ever heard you talk that much about any of it before."

"We never had five hundred screaming fans show up to a gig before," Gwen pointed out. "Look, guys. We haven't talked enough about whether we want to sign with a label or not, but whether we do or not, if we're right and this album does break big, if we start getting national coverage…" She sighed and raked her hands through her hair, knowing it would mess up the rough ponytail. "I'm not sure you really get how much it could change everything."

The others exchanged glances before Gemma said, "No, obviously we don't. You're the only one who's lived it. But we're adults, Gwen. I think we can handle it."

Gwen shook her head. "No. I mean, yeah, the popularity, I think you can, that's not a problem. It's how they're going to treat *me*. I really…" Her heart contracted, a funny sad little twist. "I really want to be a member of a band."

"Gwen." Sandy sounded exasperated. "Every band has a front man. A few of them have two, but mostly it's Josie and the Pussycats. None of us thought we'd end up being Josie when we decided to join a band with Emma Hart."

Gwen dropped her hands to stare at Sandy a moment, then at Gemma and Myles. "Did you all know who I was when you joined?"

The women all snorted, sounds that made it clear the answer was 'obviously,' while Myles, embarrassed, said, "Actually, Gemma had to tell me last year."

"Myles!" Penny's voice shot up. "You've been part of the band for three years! Are you serious?"

"Her name's Gwen!" Myles half-yelled back, still obviously embarrassed. "Why would I think she used to be Emma? There was some gig in Cheyenne," he mumbled. "A fan kept holding up a sign that said 'I HART EMMA' and after the show I asked Gemma why. She laughed at me for half an hour."

"That was *six months ago*," Sandy said incredulously. "That was *this* year!"

"Well, whatever. I didn't know."

"That's amazing and wonderful," Gwen told him honestly. "Also sorry I'm a weirdo who used to be famous and didn't tell you."

He shrugged. "It's fine. I looked you up. The really weird part was you having blonde hair. And for the record, I also didn't think I'd be Josie."

A laugh broke over the band before Sandy leaned forward in Bill's chair, making it creak. "So, yeah, Gwen, we knew. And we all respected, respect, that you didn't wanna play on being Emma Hart to break big. But...look, we've talked about this. Especially since we started recording the new album, which we all know is shit-hot. Penny is incredible at the whole social media thing and she can keep us in rotation, especially if you continue with the not doing it at all, but if we get any bigger than we are tonight, yeah, you're gonna be the lead singer, the front man for the band. And Gwen, I mean, there was a reason you were a famous kid. You've got *it*." She wet her lips and glanced at the others. Gemma nodded once, encouraging her to keep talking for the rest of them. Sandy's gaze came back to Gwen. "I guess what I'm trying to say is we know the attention is going to turn to you. We've always known that would happen if things went well. We're okay with that."

"It's just the idea of it and the reality of it are really different," Gwen said swiftly. "It's one thing to know it'll happen. It's another to watch and feel all the questions getting directed at me, the promo shots featuring me, the frickin' tabloids talking about me, the media wanting *me* on their talk shows. It's…it makes a gulf." She closed her eyes and tilted her head back again. "I remember when it happened with *Starting School*. I remember the *day* it became obvious I was the breakout star. All six of us were there, being interviewed together, ensemble cast, you know, the whole thing. And something happened, the way the interviewers kept redirecting questions to me even when one of the others was talking. The way the camera focused on me. The way they cropped everybody else out for the promo piece. And the next day after the story was out, they were all mad at me. Nobody wanted to talk to me anymore. I don't want to go through that again."

She opened her eyes to find the rest of the band glancing at each other again, and this time Gemma, who was abrupt and practical at almost all times, spoke. "We're not fourteen, Gwen." She cracked a thin smile. "I can't promise we'll be envy-free twenty-four-seven, but we're not kids. We get what we're signing up for. This isn't a pit fight."

At everyone else's startled laughter, she looked around defiantly. "Oh, come on, I can't be the only one who sees those mega-popular tween shows that way, can I? It's totally Highlander. There can be only one. They throw all these kids into a show together and see who the audiences respond to best, and the rest of them are trashed. Sometimes a bunch of them make it through, but let's be real, Gwen probably had the health-iest self-destruction of any of that crew she ended up in."

Color rushed up Gwen's face, although she couldn't really argue. She *had* self-destructed, but more or less on purpose. Two of her castmates from back then had ended up with serious drug problems, although one had made it through and still worked in film and tele-vision with regular but not breakout success. A third had simply not grown up into as cute an adult as he'd been a teen, and had retired. Gwen thought he sold real estate now. The last two had a series of high-profile disastrous relationships, including one with each other, and were still occasionally featured in 'where are they now' sob stories. Gwen hadn't fallen apart like that, and, she realized now, had some guilt about *that*, too. "You're not wrong," she said a bit faintly.

Gemma looked slightly abashed, as if she realized that might have been a little too blunt. She still said, "I know I'm not. I get where you're coming from, G. But we're not kids. It's not gonna be the same." She pulled in a deep breath, held it, then released it, saying, "Assuming you want to do this. I don't want to kid you, if you walk away I'm guessing me and Myles are probably gonna cut loose, but that's not meant as a threat. It's just we're as close to stardom as we're gonna get and it'd be stupid to not take this moment and parlay it for ourselves if you want to stay at this level."

"I don't think I do." Gwen almost surprised herself with the admission, and she could hear the quick intake of breath from her bandmates. "We've worked really hard to get where we are. I know I could have made it easier, but you've stuck with me while I took the hard road. I had stardom handed to me when I was young," she said flatly. "I was a kid and got lucky. This time I feel like maybe I've earned it. And I *know* you guys have. So, yeah, um." She gave her friends an uncertain smile. "Yeah, I mean, I think we need to talk about the label idea, but if you guys want to shoot for the stars, I'm in. And if that means a little bit of leaning into who I used to be, I can live with that, too."

"I don't think you have lean in," Penny said with a little smile of her own. "Because you're right, they're going to be all up in your face about it, but if you stick to that line—you had stardom handed to you and walked away and now you think, hope, you've earned it, Gwen Booker is the life you've chosen—then you can't stop them from waxing lyrical about Emma Hart, but you don't have to lean into it, either. And we can use Myles's story to really highlight that. Like, he basically didn't know who you used to be until we started recording the new album. Because you're good, Gwen. Because *we're* good. So the Sixty Pix are a band who look forward, not back."

Gwen burst into spontaneous applause that the others picked up on, laughter filling the little office. "You're really good at that," Gwen said as the clapping ended. "If you ever decide to stop being a rock star, you could probably have a nice job in marketing."

"Oh my God. No thanks. Come on, let's go be rock stars instead. Our fans are calling our names."

That was actually true. Gwen climbed off the floor, grinning, and pulled her bandmates into a hug, mumbling, "Thank you. Thank you all," before they headed out to the stage.

The roar of excitement that met them was too big for the size of the space. Gwen honestly thought the roof might lift off for a moment, and wondered if they should have moved the whole gig outdoors. It was too late now, and Gwen had a sudden moment of wanting to stay in the moment, clinging to it, because it might be the last time they got to play to such an intimate audience. She found Bill in the crowd—not hard, because he'd taken a stance over to one side, where his height didn't block anybody but he could see easily, and sang a couple of songs right to him. His smile lifted her in ways she hadn't known was possible, and when the show was over and he came back to scoop her into a congratulatory hug, she whispered, "You're gonna escort me out and steal me away from all of this, right?"

His laugh was almost inaudible, but she felt it rumbling through her body. "Yeah. But I'm going to bring you back, too, because this is what you're meant to do. I'm just lucky enough to be here to see it."

She beamed up at him. It was ridiculous to think how *right* that felt when she'd only known the man a couple of days, but it felt right anyway, filling her heart with joy. "Perfect. That sounds perfect." A pang shot through her as she realized she was leaving the next day, although Gwen reminded herself she'd be back next weekend: they already had a date planned. One less chaotic than this weekend had been. At least in theory.

It took forever to get through the waiting crowds, but every minute was worth it. Gwen was still flying with exuberance when they finally broke free, which turned out to mean 'went back to the pub so they could escape out the back door.' Bill's truck was waiting, and he went to the gentlemanly effort of opening the door for her. "Your place or mine?"

"Oh, yours!" Gwen said, startled. "I forgot you lived here. Yeah, yours. That way the hotel won't have any noise complaints."

Bill, beneath his breath but loud enough to hear, said, "Oh my God," and Gwen laughed.

"I can probably be quiet if you want me t—"

"Nope! No, no thank you, that won't be necessary. But forgive me for being glad I only live a few blocks away." They were more or less at his house by the time the conversation ended, in fact, and he said, "Stay there," in a tone that sounded more helpful than commanding. A moment later he was at her door again, lifting her down from the truck, although nowhere near *all* the way down. He wrapped her legs around his waist, her skirt rucking up around her hips, and leaned her up against the side of the truck, lowering his mouth to hers and kissing her thoroughly before mumbling, "I currently regret my decision to live in town. If I'd gotten that place out in the woods we would already be having sex."

"It's very late," Gwen said hopefully. "I can be very quiet. No one will know."

"Mmm, no, I definitely want someone to know. You. Me. But not the neighbors." He moved away from the truck, still effortlessly holding her, and closed its door before carrying her up to the house. Gwen twisted, trying to get a look as he opened the door— unlocked it, holding her just as effortlessly with one hand under her ass instead of two—and stepped inside.

It was, of course, dark, and he didn't bother turning a light on. That was fine: Gwen was plenty turned on for anybody or anything. She did grin and murmur, "Nice place," against his mouth, and Bill laughed.

"Thanks. I tidied up just for you."

"And I wore a skirt just for you."

Bill groaned. "I noticed. You didn't warn me about the thigh-high boots. You were the sexiest woman I've ever seen up there on stage. Do you have to take the boots off?"

"Do you want me to?"

He shuddered, grabbing her ass more firmly and pulsing his hips against hers. "I really fucking don't. Bedroom?"

"I don't really care as long as you don't put me down."

He murmured, "Gwen," and captured her mouth with his again, this time with slow intensity that left her aching throughout for more of his touch. His hand slid up her spine, pushing her shirt out of the way until she lifted her arms so he could pull it all the way off, all without having to put her down. He glanced down at the mounds of her breasts in their bra, and groaned again. "Black lace. You're trying to kill me." He was good at unfastening a bra with one hand; it loosened and she discarded it with a laugh, kissing him and winding her arms around his neck.

"I'm almost sure killing is *not* what I'm trying to do. God, you're so strong. How the hell can you just hold me up like this?"

"I'm very strong," he replied, amused. "You like it?"

"So much," she whispered. "You make me feel fragile and very fuckable." She kissed his throat, rucking his own shirt up so she could run her hands over the solid muscle of his chest, and shivered. "God, you're *big*. Oh, how am I going to get this off you!" It took a moment of effort on both their parts before his shirt joined hers on the floor. Gwen had the vague idea they'd gone down a hallway, but she had no idea if they were heading for a bedroom or a kitchen counter. She squirmed her hand down between their bodies, finding the fly of his jeans, and Bill took a sharp, deep breath.

"If you spend much time down there I'm going to forget entirely about foreplay," he warned.

"That's not the discouragement you think it is," she whispered back. "I've been thinking about you all day. I'm plenty warmed up."

He breathed, "Gwen," as she undid his fly and pushed his jeans down with her heels, making sure to take his shorts with them. Bill took another half step, froze, and made a sound of frustrated desire. "I'm going to kill us both if I keep heading for the bedroom. Jeans are around my ankles. I'll trip."

"As long as you can keep holding me, here is *real* good," Gwen promised breathily.

"I will *never* let you fall. Gwen, can I, I want to, I need you, can I?"

She whispered, "You better," and shuddered as he shifted her position against him a little, her boot-clad thighs around his hips instead of his waist as he slid into her, with a rough chuckle and an adjustment for the tiny panties she hadn't taken off. Gwen, thickly, said, "Oh my God. Oh my God, you *are* big," and to her shock, orgasmed abruptly from the pleasure of being claimed so gently by so much size. "Bill, *yes*, Jesus!"

"Ah God." He laughed, clutching her to him, and buried his face in her shoulder a moment before finding her mouth for more kisses. "God, you feel good, Gwen. God, yeah." She felt him stepping out of the jeans, leaving them behind as he adjusted his grip on her, settling her more comfortably and then sliding his thumb down her spine so she arched abruptly. He ducked his head to catch one of her nipples in his mouth and heat spilled through her again, erupting in a cry of pleasure that made him tighten his grip around her waist. "Oh *yeah*."

"Oh my God," she said again, somewhere between laughter and stupidity. "You're so big. So strong. Oh my *God*, Bill. Yeah. Again. More. More?" She was lost in his strength, flying again, pleasure coursing through her as they moved together. As he moved them through the house, too, although slowly, until he suddenly sat down somewhere and her own weight drove her more deeply onto him as he no longer carried it the same way. Gwen came again, crying out with release, and he slid his fingers between their bodies to work her clit as he thrust up into her, until another orgasm made her shriek and beg for him to come with her.

He groaned and heat spilled into her like he'd been waiting for permission, the thick throbs pulsing against her in the most satisfying ways. She collapsed against him, gasping and struggling to catch her breath between kisses, and shivered from the bones out. Bill whispered, "Perfect," against her hair, and for a little while, everything was.

CHAPTER 26

Gwen Booker in his arms was the only thing Bill ever wanted, except maybe Gwen Booker in his arms with the lights on. He mumbled that eventually, and at her laughing assent, reached down the couch to switch a lamp on. She winced a complaint, but with her eyes half-lidded against the light, slid her hands down his chest and murmured awe. "Big man. Big muscle. I like it. You."

He chuckled and gathered her closer, as if she could get much closer, burying his face in her shoulder for a moment, then sliding his hands around her body to cup her breasts. "Speaking of big. Don't mean to be rude, but where were you hiding this under those t-shirts?"

"More under the leather jackets," she said with a smile. "I thought you knew."

"I figured it out as soon as the bra came off." He dipped his head to kiss the tops of her breasts, encouraging her to arch back so he could use his mouth and fingers until she was gasping and squirming against him. "Still have a problem," he murmured. "I really want to see you in nothing but those boots and also really don't want to move you."

Her laughter was warm and trembling against his skin. She straightened up a bit, reached behind her, and unzipped the skirt. Unzipped it all the way, as it turned out: a couple seconds later she held up a band of leather that had once been a skirt, and dropped it beside them on the couch. Bill breathed a prayer, then slid his fingertips beneath the waistband of a very, *very* tiny pair of black lace panties. "How attached to these are you?"

"…I can get more?"

"I like that answer." He tested the elastic with his fingertips again, then brought his other hand around to her hip and with a quick jerk, popped the waistband. It snapped. Gwen shrieked, her whole body tensing up in surprise, which, given where she was sitting, turned Bill cross-eyed for a moment. When he found his voice, it was to say, "This is already working out better than I imagined," before snapping the other hip's elastic. Gwen startled again, and Bill shivered, sliding the tiny panties out of the way and then his hands over her hips. "Ah, *God*, yeah. Do you have any idea how gorgeous you are?"

"Maybe you just have a thing for women in tall boots riding your cock."

He twitched so hard he thought he might come again, and pulled her deeper onto himself as he lifted his hips as he said, "Jesus, Gwen," in a thick voice.

She leaned in, nuzzling his throat. "So the responsible son likes a little dirty talk, hm?"

"I like your dirty talk," he said, still hoarsely. She was paler-skinned than he was, blue undertones instead of his golden ones, and her black-dyed hair was an incredible contrast to that paleness. She had broader shoulders than he'd realized, which also helped disguise her bustiness, which he now sort of thought of as his own personal secret. He lifted his hands to her breasts again, tugging and brushing at her nipples and watching them flush pink as her breath went short. She had a small waist: he'd known that from her short-cropped shirts, and her hips were more slender than he would have expected. She had a little line of flowery tattoos from her bellybutton downward, matched by curved ones over her hip bones, like they were all helpfully leading to the little thatch of dark gold curls between her thighs. He'd known she dyed her hair. Seeing the proof that cuffs and collar didn't match made him harder than he'd thought possible. Most of her legs were swallowed by the long leather boots, but the contrast of pale flesh and black leather there was as enticing as her hair and skin were. "God, you're beautiful."

"Know what else I am? Flexible." Gwen caught his hand to give herself an anchor, then leaned backward until she was lying back across—almost between, because they were spread—his thighs. Bill grabbed her hip, making sure she didn't slide off him, and she almost purred, releasing his other hand to her other hip. "Good boy. Don't let me fall." Then her fingers slipped between her own thighs as he watched, and he found himself pounding into her, hands knotted on her hips as she worked herself, voice rising in pleasure. There was no way he could hold out when her orgasm slammed through her, and in its aftermath he dragged her back up into his arms, gasping and holding on. When she'd caught her breath again, it was to murmur, "Wait until you see the tattoos on the *other* side," and give a quiet, wicked laugh.

Bill thought he might have died and gone to heaven. His voice was actually shaking as he breathed, "Maybe you better not show me those tonight," and she laughed again, stealing a kiss.

"Gotta save something for next weekend. Or the morning, at least." She nuzzled in some more, warm and soft. "Maybe we should go to the actual bedroom?"

"I can't promise that won't lead to looking at the rest of your tattoos." Bill stood anyway, keeping her with him, and she clenched and shuddered again.

"*God* but I like that. You're so big. Nobody's ever just been able to lift me before."

"I live to serve."

Gwen purred. "Don't tempt me by saying things like that, big man."

"If you don't mind, I think I might spend the rest of my life trying to tempt you." Bill brought her to the bedroom, ghosting his hand over one of her boots as he sat on the edge of the bed with her. "I'm kind of guessing you don't want to sleep in these."

"Not unless you want to wake up to very smelly feet," she admitted reluctantly, then gave him a sweet, lazy grin. "Next time I'll find something more breathable."

"Make no changes on my account," he informed her firmly. They did, eventually, peel the boots off and sleep, although Bill got a glimpse of the tattoos on her back that made sleeping, and other things, hard. On the other hand, they both needed the rest, and he was awake before Gwen, so rose to make breakfast. Coffee and cinnamon rolls from a tube, since he didn't want to leave the house to get fresh ones from the bakery, but their scent called Gwen to wobble out of the bedroom sleepily, wearing one of his shirts and a sweet smile.

"I see you've learned everything you need to know about the care and feeding of a Gwen," she said as she sat down with the little breakfast.

Bill laughed. "I sincerely doubt that, but hopefully I'm off to a good start."

"I think so." She gave him a surprisingly shy smile, given the activities they'd been up to all night. "Does that mean you still want me to come out this weekend?"

"It really means I'd like you to never leave," he said, maybe too honestly, "but yes, please. I very much do."

She laughed and stretched a leg out to touch his shin with her toes under the table. "I *can* work remotely, but I'm not sure my boss would appreciate me just never showing up in the office again. Also, never is a long time. You might get tired of banging a rock star."

Bill coughed on his coffee. "Unlikely. Anybody who gets tired of banging a rock star probably needs their head examined. But…" He drew a deep, nervous breath. "I don't want to be completely overwhelming—"

"Then you probably shouldn't have proven you did not, in fact, need a wall to put me up against while having stand-up sex," Gwen said with a grin that faded as he ducked his head, smiling uncertainly. "Ah, no, I see, I'm supposed to be serious now. Okay. It can't possibly be more overwhelming than 'I turn into a bear,' and I think I went with that one pretty well."

"You did." He looked up again with another smile. "It's related to that, though."

"Oh my God." Gwen's eyes widened hopefully. "Can you show me how to turn into a bear?"

Surprise shot through him and came out as a laugh. "No. Sorry, no. It's inherent."

"In-bear-ent?"

He stared at her flatly enough that Gwen threw her head back and laughed. "Oh, come on, that was pretty good."

"That was awful!"

"That's what pretty good is, in puns! Okay, okay, tell me the overwhelming thing."

"The other important thing about being a shifter is we know when we've met the person we're meant to be with," Bill blurted, afraid he'd lose his nerve if he thought about it even an instant longer. "We call it finding our mate, but it's really—it's just—it's—"

Gwen's expression had gone surprised, then so, so soft. "Love at first sight?" she asked very quietly.

Bill nodded, still nervous. "A love we're absolutely certain about, but…yeah."

"And your, uh, your 'mates,' they feel it too?" At his second nod, Gwen bit her lip. "And that's us?"

"It is," Bill said in a very soft voice. "I know it's a lot and it doesn't mean we have to be together forever now, but I wanted you to know that I...I'll always be here for you, Gwen."

"That's such a relief," she said over his last words, then blushed. "I mean, that's great too, but I meant, I've been feeling so at home, so comfortable, and, yeah, so incredibly attracted to you. With you. Like everything's going to be okay now that I've met you. And I thought I was probably losing my mind, but it's...magic?"

Bill blinked. "I wouldn't have thought of it quite like that, but yeah, I guess it is."

"You turn into a bear," Gwen pointed out. "That's definitely in the 'magic' category. So is love at first sight." She sighed, then sighed again and sank her teeth into a cinnamon roll before looking dreamily at him. "I have *no* idea how we're going to work this out. You've got a pub to run and I'm apparently on the verge of *oh!*" She sat up straight, staring at him accusingly. "Is that why I'm finally okay with the idea of hitting the big time? Because I subconsciously *know* I'll be okay because I've got you on my side?"

"It might be," Bill said, surprised. "Is that okay?"

"It's amazing! It makes sense! I know I've been playing it safe, but—wow." Gwen's voice softened. "Wow. God, Bill. You're right. This is a lot. Not a bad kind of lot," she said quickly, "but a lot."

"It is." He reached across the table toward her, ignoring the fact that he had cinnamon roll stickiness on his fingers. Again. "Which is why I said we don't have to make all the decisions right now. I just really wanted you to know I'd be in your corner."

She curled her fingers into his. "If this album does well—we'll be touring anyway, but if it does well we might be touring a lot. For quite a while. That can be months apart, Bill. And I know we've only spent three days together, but months apart sounds like a lot, too."

"Well." He took a deep breath, then chuckled at himself. "I'm fortifying myself with a lot of deep breathing these days. You?"

"So much." Gwen flashed a smile. "I should become a yogi or something, that's how much. What were you going to say?"

"I talked to my parents about the pub last night. I'm going to hire my cousin Ashley to run the actual pub side of things, if I can convince her I mean it. The brewery needs less day to day supervision, but…if I need somebody to take over there, too, I'll find them, and step back into some other kind of position. Because yeah, months sounds like too long. And I've never traveled." He gave her a sudden nervous smile. "I mean, if you'd want me around."

"More than anything. Although Penny is going to lecture you about sex before game day."

Bill burst out laughing. "Isn't the problem with that the staying up too late thing? I promise to only have morning sex after you've awakened from your fabulous nights as a rock star? Or very, very late night sex after which you can sleep in until," he checked the time, "eleven thirty a.m?"

"I'll have you know I'm up unusually early after a night of rock'n'roll and sex, because *somebody* made cinnamon rolls and drew me from my bed long before my natural hour of awakening."

"So you're saying if I'm going to go on tour with you and want to do actual tourist things, I should get up early, go do the stuff, and come back around one in the afternoon to worship my rock and roll queen until it's time for her to go bathe in the adoration of her countless fans?"

Gwen pursed her lips. "I think you're going to be very good at this."

Bill grinned. "I'm going to try. In the meantime, since I got you up so early—"

"I would love to go back to bed and get thoroughly railed again."

Heat flashed up Bill's face. "I was going to ask if you wanted to go over to the pub with me and try to talk Ashley into actually taking the job I offered her twice yesterday."

"Oh." Gwen settled herself into the kitchen chair quite primly, like an embarrassed cat. "That sounds okay, too."

"Shower first?"

All the embarrassed cat body language went away, replaced by something close to a purr from his fated mate. "Now that sounds like an excellent compromise."

A few minutes later, beneath the hot water, they concluded that it absolutely was.

CHAPTER 27

The pub had that 'aftermath-of-a-party' vibe to it, Gwen thought. It had been cleaned up —no sad streamers or deflated balloons in the corners, no paper plates or red plastic cups piled anywhere, not that there would have been anyway because it hadn't been that kind of party—but it seemed sort of tired and echoey and empty.

Although honestly, there were quite a few people there for an early Sunday afternoon. A lot of them were Torben family members—and they all looked *exhausted,* which might have been why Gwen thought the whole place had a tired, afterparty air to it—but there were a number of patrons, too. She suspected some were people from the gigs who were hoping to catch a glimpse of her, but as long as they were at the pub, spending their money, that seemed just fine. And some of them *didn't* have an "I've been partying all weekend" aura to them: they were just cheerful afternoon patrons, a trio of whom were twenty-somethings wondering why they'd never been there before.

"I thought it was for old people," one of them said. "I drink their beer at a couple of the bars downtown, but I thought this *place* was for old people, you know? But I guess it was party central all weekend so I gotta put it on my list of places to watch for gigs and stuff."

"I couldn't get tickets," another said morosely. "I was at the Harlequin on Thursday but by the time I went to the ticket site, the gigs for the pub were sold out."

Gwen grinned up at Bill, put her finger over her lips, then went and slid into the free seat in the booth the trio of twenty-somethings. "Hey, sorry for being rude and interrupting, but how was the Harlequin gig?"

The young man she'd sat down next to said, "Oh, it was gre*holy shit*!" with the last two words at such volume the whole pub fell silent. He turned red. The young woman across the table turned even redder and put her face in her hands. The third, another young man, just sat silently, gaping at Gwen, and then in a fit of brilliance, lifted his phone to take a picture of her huge cheesy grin and his friend's red, red face. The guy at her side said, "Oh my God, you asshole, don't post that—" and the guy across from her said, "Too late!"

Gwen, beaming, said, "I'm glad you enjoyed the show," and got up and left to the sounds of their agonized protestations. She went back, laughing, to get pictures with all of them, and then left them to their business, which she was fairly certain would be incoherent squealing for the next while.

Bill watched the whole thing with a look of bemusement, as did a number of the other Torben clan members. "So this is my life now," he murmured into her hair, and Gwen shrugged up at him cheerfully.

"This is the fun part of it, yeah. Lots of it is less cool, but yeah. Ashley!" She waved vigorously at the young woman. "Bill says you're basically single-handedly responsible for the service going so well over the weekend. When he hires you as the general manager, demand a raise immediately."

"I'm already offering her a built-in raise!"

"She needs another one!"

"How about a Christmas bonus?"

Gwen pursed her lips. "Okay, I can work with that." She beamed at Ashley. "I'm sure it was chaos from the floor side of things but it was amazing from the performance side, so good job, and thank you, and when are you starting officially?"

"I was just helping out. I mean, sure, I'd love to." The young woman shrugged, looking embarrassed. "But, you know, it's Bill's pub."

"And I've been trying all weekend to hire you!"

"Wait, really? I mean, you've been serious?" Ashley's eyes widened. "Really?"

Bill gestured her toward a booth, and all three of them went to sit down together, Ashley still agape. "I'm absolutely serious. I talked to my parents about it yesterday. You were right, Ash. I'm doing two jobs here, and I literally haven't even *been* to the actual brewery in days. And—I haven't told most of the family yet, but," he lowered his voice, "Gwen is my mate."

Gwen, under her breath, said, "I can't believe you call true loves your *mates*," and rolled her eyes, which got a glimpse of a smile out of Ashley, but the young woman was too busy gawking between Bill and Gwen to really laugh at the comment.

"*Really*? Oh my God. Congratulations! But—oooh!" Ashley's eyes widened again. "So that's…oh, that's why you want a general manager? Because maybe you'll be, like, not here?"

"I want a general manager because I don't like running a pub," Bill said wryly. "Not really. And you said you've got a vision for it. Well, let's sit down with Mom and Dad and talk about your vision and your salary. But also yes. Because I might not be here as much."

Ashley bounced in the booth, clapping her hands but trying to keep it small and quiet. "Oh my God. That's amazing. For you guys, I mean! Not for me! Also for me. But much less so! Congratulations! Oh my God," she added again to Gwen. "How'd you take it? The whole, you know, raar." She made claws out of her fingers and bared her teeth.

"I hid behind a bench and swore a lot," Gwen said with dignity, then quirked her eyebrows downward. "And then I was okay, actually. What's that about? How do you make the adjustment from," she also dropped her voice, "'holy shit he's a bear' to 'oh ok he's a bear' in like ninety seconds?"

The two shifters—she assumed, anyway, that Ashley was a shifter, but if she wasn't, she certainly knew about them—both blinked at her, then at each other. "It must be part of the magic," Bill said after a moment. "I never thought about it. Mates just always seem to come to terms with it pretty easily."

"Of course." Gwen shook her head and smiled. "I should have realized."

Bill, more able to stay on point, said, "Can we talk about it? You as general manager here? Not right now if you don't want to, but pretty soon?"

"I would love that." Ashley beamed. "Yeah, I'd love that, if you're sure. Ooh, I have *plans*. Okay, I'm gonna go write up a business plan. Congratulations again!" She bounced out of the booth and strode off toward the office, leaving Gwen and Bill to smile after her.

"That's going to work out well for you," Gwen said at the same time Bill said, "I wonder what her plans are." They both laughed, and he added, "She's got a business degree, so I imagine her plan is going to look very official. I'm almost afraid."

"I have a degree in music composition," Gwen said, still looking after Ashley. "I could not write a business plan with it."

"No, but you could apparently write a chart-topping rock ballad with it, and I bet Ashley can't do that. I went to college for a brewing degree."

"They have those?" Gwen asked, astonished. "For real?"

"For real. You can even get a Masters degree in it, but I didn't finish the course. I was still doing the faires then and it was more fun to do that from April through October than go to school."

Gwen laughed. "A crack shows in his responsibility armor?"

"More like it hadn't finished forming yet, I think." He smiled at her.

"Oh," she said, thoughts bouncing ahead, "oh, that makes sense though. Not the responsibility armor, but Ashley's got a business degree and you went to school to learn to be a better brewmaster. Your heart's really not in the pub at all. Did you even realize that?"

Bill hesitated, then blinked. "No. Not when you put it that way, no. I thought brewmaster, pub, it all made sense. Although I didn't know I was going to end up running the pub, then. Look at you." He grinned. "Fated mate, coming along and making sense of my whole life."

"Look at you," she said back to him. "Fated mate, still can't believe you call it that but moving on, coming along and giving me the support and confidence I need to move on with my life."

"You had the confidence," he disagreed.

Gwen's eyebrows rose. "Not sure I did, but even if we leave it at support, it's a big deal, big man. I haven't talked to the band yet—"

Bill laughed. "Yeah, I'm aware. We've been joined at the hip since the gig ended last night."

Gwen leered. "Yeah we have. In the best possible way, too. *Any*way. But I did text them to see if we could have a talk this afternoon about whether we want to sign with your friend Mike's label. Is there somewhere we can hang out where we're not right in the public eye like we are here?"

"Yeah, the event room." Bill tilted his head toward a part of the pub Gwen hadn't been in. "I'll show you. You think you'll sign with him?"

"I don't know. On one hand, it's giving a third party some of our income. On the other, if he's good at his job, it could really catapult us. So we'll have to talk about it." Gwen nudged his hip with her own. "Scoot, big guy. Let's go get some cinnamon rolls to soften up the band with."

"You do know we serve food here, right? Quite good food, actually? Award-winning and everything?"

"Yes, but do you serve cinnamon rolls?"

"Well." Bill sighed theatrically. "No. No, we don't. All right, to the bakery, then. You want to take the Impala or my truck?"

"They're both in the back lot now anyway, so let's toss a coin when we get there." Gwen slid her hand into Bill's and let him lead her through the pub toward the back door. A number of Torbens winked or waved at them, and she said, "Who *did* you tell about this whole mates thing, because I think everybody knows now."

"I may have mentioned it to my parents."

Gwen laughed. "Oh. Yeah. Okay. Everybody knows. Ashley must have been late to the family gossip chat."

"Even I am," Bill confessed. "I've barely looked at it over the weekend. I think it's been good for me." He pushed the back door open to a blast of cooler air, and shot a look at the mountains. "We don't need winter yet, dammit."

"Then you shouldn't live in Colorado." Gwen smiled

up at him, then glanced past him toward her car. There was somebody leaning on it: an older man, white, baseball cap and a jeans jacket over a t-shirt and jeans. She yelled, "Hey!" in immediate outrage. "Get the hell off my car!"

The guy stood up immediately, swiping his baseball cap off to reveal thinning brown hair and an ingratiating smile. "Hey, sweetheart."

Gwen recoiled internally, but that didn't stop her furious forward motion. She stalked past Bill, which took some effort: he was striding toward the Impala, too, and he had much longer legs than Gwen did. She snarled, "I'm not your fucking sweetheart, asshole," at the stranger. "Whatever the hell you think you're do—"

"Gwen," the guy interrupted. "Gwen, baby. It's me. It's your Daddy."

THE WORLD FELL out from under Gwen's feet so hard and fast she would have collapsed if Bill hadn't been right there, slipping an arm around her waist. She looked down, making sure the asphalt parking lot surface was still actually *there*, because it really didn't feel like it. It was, which almost didn't make sense.

It made more sense than the thin asshole at her car being her *father*, though. She looked up again, shaking with rage, confusion, and adrenaline as she stared at the guy.

It took entire seconds before he snapped into place,

recognizable as the man she'd last seen fifteen years ago. Ike Booker was thinner than he'd been, obviously older, dressed far more casually than she could remember seeing him for almost her entire childhood. He wore glasses, which he hadn't before, but the ingratiating, too-white smile was the same. Her income had paid for that smile, both the straightness of his teeth and the veneers that made it so bright.

For a long few seconds, that was all Gwen could think, looking at him: she'd paid for his teeth. She'd been eleven and had done a series of commercials, and he'd used most of her paychecks to get his teeth done. It would help her career, he'd said. The better-looking and more professional *he* was, the more seriously he, and by extension, *she*, would be taken.

The bitter thing was, he may well have been right. But now all Gwen could think was, she'd paid for those teeth, and in exchange, her father had disappeared with every penny she'd ever made.

He was beaming at her with that bright, bright smile. He even opened his arms for a hug. Bill, at Gwen's side, growled so deep in his chest she thought he might actually turn into a bear.

Part of her wanted that more than anything in the entire world. It would be so amazing to watch him shift into that huge grizzly and swat the asshole who called himself her father right into oblivion.

But that would be really, really bad for the shifter community. The last thing she wanted was for Bill, and maybe his whole family and who knew how many others, to be outed, just because her knees had stopped working.

All at once they were working again. Gwen stalked forward, straight up to her father like she'd return the embrace but with her fists balled.

At the absolute last second, she remembered a fight scene she'd had choreographed in one of the few movies she'd done as a kid, and instead of literally punching him, she thrust the heel of her hand straight into her father's nose, and felt a shockingly satisfying *crunch* before he screamed and doubled over in pain, clutching at his face. "You crazy bitch! What the hell! What the fuck, Gwen? What the actual fuck?!"

Gwen wiped blood onto her jeans and whispered, "Gross. I didn't think that through," before getting her phone out with shaking hands. "Bill, can you hold him please. I'm calling the police."

"Yeah, you call the police, you crazy bitch, I'm gonna have you up on assault!" Her father make a *glerk*ing sound at the end of that, as Bill, with extreme calm and ease, wrapped a big hand around the back of his neck and held on. "Get your fucking hands off me!"

"I think," Gwen said, as calmly as she could, "that the police will be more interested in the *fifteen million dollars* you stole from me. Yeah, hi," she said into the phone as Bill's gaze snapped to her and he mouthed 'fifteen *million?*' in visible shock. "Hi, I need an officer or something at the Thunder Bear Brewpub. My name is Emma Hart and I've just found the man who stole every penny I'd ever made."

There was a shocked silence on the other end of the

line before the woman who'd answered said, "Emma Hart from *Starting School*?"

Gwen inhaled through her nose. She hadn't introduced herself that way in a very, very long time. But she nodded now and said, "That's the one."

The woman's voice rose. "*You found your dad?*"

"I did," Gwen said after another deep breath. She'd used her stage name because she wanted to be recognized, just this once. It didn't make it any less weird to have a random stranger know the details of her life. "He's currently being restrained in the back parking lot of the Thunder Bear Brewpub. He'll probably want to press assault charges. I think I broke his nose."

The woman muttered, "Good for you," and then cleared her throat. "I mean, I'll have an officer sent right away, Ms. Hart."

Gwen said, "Thank you," and hung up, only then allowing herself to become aware that her father was still swearing and dripping blood on the asphalt. She stared at him a long moment, trying to slow her heartbeat. It didn't work: she was cold, sweaty, and sick to her stomach. "Have you been in Renaissance all along?"

"What the hell does that matter, you *crazy bi*—"

Bill tightened his hand on the back of her father's neck. "I would watch my language if I were you, Mr. Booker."

"It doesn't matter," Gwen said quietly. "Bill, I'm really sorry to do this to you, but—"

"Go," he said immediately. "It's okay. I can handle this guy." The last two words dripped with disgust. "Go find my parents. They'll take care of you until the cops get here. And Gwen?"

She hesitated, already on her way inside, but looking back. Bill smiled. "I love you."

The ice in her chest burst in a flash of heat and joy, and all of a sudden, despite her father, everything was all right. "I love you too."

She fled inside.

CHAPTER 28

Her father was still howling, "That bitch broke my nose!" when the cops took him away less than an hour later. Gwen was almost certain she hadn't actually broken it, and the officer on duty apologetically told her that she might be up on a misdemeanor assault charge whether she had or hadn't.

"But," the officer said almost cheerfully, "it's a first offense, and you can probably get a defense for heat of passion to knock it down to a fine, if the judge even goes that far. I'd have punched the son of a bitch, too. Not that I told you that."

"I didn't hear anything," Gwen promised in a whisper. She hadn't wanted to come back out for the arrest, but she was the victim in the larger crime, so she kind of had to. Bill's family had absorbed her into compassionate silence when she'd explained what was going on, and in the aftermath of her father's arrest, Bill wrapped her in his arms. He didn't ask, or even say anything, and after a long, shivering moment, she whispered, "I'm okay. I think."

His arms tightened around her. "Wanna go back inside?" At her nod, he walked her slowly back into the building, and spoke over her head to his family, who were all still clustered in the events room. "Could somebody get Gwen an Irish coffee?"

"That sounds amazing," Gwen whispered. Half his family immediately headed out to the bar, and the rest backed off, giving her, and Bill, space. Gwen couldn't help a very quiet laugh. "I'm going to have a whole lineup of Irish coffees, I guess. I'm okay," she said a little more strongly to the remaining family. "Thank you for..." She trailed off, looking at the four tall people in the room, and found an actual smile. "For all being so large and reassuring. Honestly I thought Bill was going to—"

She broke off, suddenly unsure of how open she should be about his ability to turn into a bear, but Bill picked up with a rumbling laugh. "It's a good thing you punched him. I was about to shift and knock him into the mountains."

"Part of me really wanted you to," Gwen admitted in a soft rush. "But I'm glad you didn't. It would have been more trouble for you than it was worth."

"I knew him," Heather, Bill's mother, said in distress. "Not well, but he used to come into the pub sometimes. I'm so sorry, Gwen."

"He changed his name," Gwen pointed out. "There's no reason you could have guessed. It's all right. He just..." She wanted to sit down all of a sudden, and Bill, as if sensing it, led her to the couches. Gwen collapsed, face in her hands until there was a faint *thunk* on the table in front of her, and the scent of whiskey-flavored coffee rose to her nostrils. "Oh, God, thank you." She lifted the drink and sipped, wincing at the heat, but the combination of caffeine, alcohol and sugar was honestly soothing right then. "That's good. Thank you."

Someone made a pleased noise in response, and Gwen had another couple sips before feeling fortified enough to look up at Bill's nervously gathered family. A giggle broke from her chest. "Look at you all, looming."

"What's going *on*?" Penny's voice rose over the gathering, and the Torbens parted to let the arriving band members see Gwen on the couch. Penny's entire body radiated worry. "Somebody out front told us that Gwen's *dad* showed up? Are you okay, hon? What the hell is happening? Did he really show up? Did you kick him in the fucking nuts?"

"I punched him in the face," Gwen offered.

A huge grin split Penny's face. "*Amazing.* Excellent. That's perfect. What the hell happened?" She crowded through to sit next to Gwen, opposite Bill, who still had his arm around her. "Are you okay?"

"I am. I think I am. He's been living here for years under an assumed name," Gwen said with a nod toward Heather. "I'm almost sure it's going to turn out he's burned through everything he stole. I think he saw the ads for the shows this weekend and decided he'd come back and get more money out of me."

Penny, blankly, said, "But you don't have any money," which made Gwen laugh.

"He doesn't know that, though. And if things go well with this album…"

"Then *he* still won't have any money. I hope he rots in jail for the rest of his miserable life. Do people do that for stealing money these days?"

"If they're not really rich to begin with, yeah," someone else muttered, and a low grumbling chuckle went around the whole group. Bill's family began to filter out of the room, heads ducked together so they could gossip quietly. Gwen figured they'd be gossiping forever about this, and made a face.

"Oh, God. This is going to hit the news in a big way."

Myles cleared his throat. "The album's ready."

The whole band looked at him, varying degrees of confusion on their faces, although Gemma started to smirk even before he shrugged. "I'm just saying. We don't *have* to wait until next year to release it. It's ready now. And you're about to be a news story."

Sandy, after a pause, said, "You mean there's no such thing as bad publicity. Here's Gwen Booker, AKA Emma Hart, whose dad stole her life savings and drove her into retirement at age eighteen—"

Gwen mumbled, "That's not really what I did," but Sandy was gaining steam and ignored her.

"—and now he's been arrested for fraud or embezzlement or whatever it is, and Gwen's back with a new album, and *everybody* is going to want to interview her. It's a gold mine for publicity. We couldn't *pay* for that kind of publicity."

"We also can't get physical media ready for release

that fast!" Gwen protested. "We could release it digitally, yeah, but even if we fulfilled physical orders ourselves we don't have anywhere to print or warehouse it!"

"We don't," Gemma said with a sharkish grin, "but Mike Piccolo does."

Another startled silence swept the band before Penny cackled. "Soooooo we're signing with a label, then?"

All eyes, including Bill's, turned to Gwen. "Oh my God. This is not a me-alone decision!"

"Let me, I don't have an oar in this race," Bill said. Everyone stared at him, and he cringed, although he did so with a laugh. "Horse in this race. Oar in this boat. Something! I don't have one, anyway! Hands up, all in favor of signing with Harlequin Renaissance Records?"

Four hands shot into the air, and Gwen, grinning so hard she thought she might cry, lifted hers, too. "Yeah," she whispered, completely overcome. "Yeah, let's do this thing."

A cheer almost knocked her over, and then Penny *did* knock her over with a hug. All at once there was a dogpile of hugs and cheers and tears, everybody sort of squishing Bill, who had ended up at the bottom of the pile and who said, "It's okay, I'm big, I like bear hugs, I can take it," in a distant voice that made the whole band break down into giggles.

"You better be able to," Gwen said, trying to steal a kiss. "I don't think I can do this without you."

Gemma, somewhere in the dogpile, said, "Oh, gross.

You can obviously do it without him. You can't do it without *us*. *We're* the band!"

"Right, right, my mistake." Except Gwen knew it wasn't a mistake. In just a few days, Bill Torben had changed her life. Maybe she *could* do this without him, but she absolutely didn't want to. Still *oof*ing and grunting as people tried to extract themselves from the dogpile of a hug, she murmured, "So if it's okay I might just stick around this week, instead of heading back to Denver and coming over to Renaissance for the weekend?"

"What about the day job?" Bill's smile was right there, kissable and bright.

"Told you they'll let me work remotely sometimes. I'm sure they'll understand. I mean, how often does somebody find the love of their life *and* get a breakout album in one weekend?"

"Wait a minute, wait a minute, wait a minute. Love of your life? What? You're breaking my heart?" Penny demanded as she squirmed out of the hug with an injured-enough expression that Gwen saw terror flash across Bill's face before Penny began to laugh. "Oh my God, your face. No, I'm sorry, I'm just kidding. We've been watching you two make starry eyes at each other all weekend, so I'm glad you've made it official after, what, seventy-two hours?"

Gwen, with some effort, dug her phone out of her jeans pocket and checked the time, which was just after two in the afternoon. "Yep. Three days, pretty much to the minute."

"I need three days like that," Penny announced. "You

and Bill, Gemma and Myles…" She trailed off and eyed Sandy. "I guess that leaves you and me, kid."

Sandy wrinkled her nose and, delicately, said, "Ew. No offense, but ew. All of that stuff is ew."

Penny flopped dramatically on the couch. "Gwen and Bill, Gemma and Myles, an ace guitarist, and poooooooor Penny all on her own."

"Poor Penny is going to be fighting off the fans in a few months," Gemma promised without a hint of sympathy. "Suck it up until then."

"Man, with these kinds of friends, who needs enemies?"

The band kept bantering as Gwen tucked herself up against Bill's side. "You know it's not just going to be my life that gets a little crazy," she said quietly. "You sure you want to be neck-deep in this? *Trust* me, I know how weird celebrity life can be."

"If it gets too much for me on the road I've got a brewery to run here." Bill smiled down at her. "I've got a brewery to run here anyway. If you end up touring, I do want to come along for as much of that as I possibly can, but I don't think I'm constitutionally capable of just dumping all my responsibilities here to become a roadie."

"I wouldn't want you to," Gwen admitted with a smile of her own. "I think I like this responsible streak you've got. It makes me feel grounded, and that feels good."

"Then I'd say we'll work it out." Bill dipped his head to kiss her, and Gwen sighed happily as he added,

"Crazy is fine, as long as it ends up with us together. I'm looking forward to seeing how it all goes."

"Me too. As long as it goes to, like, Madison Square Garden along the way. I've always wanted to play there."

Bill laughed out loud. "Great. I don't think I can afford to buy a sponsorship there, though, so you're going to have to drink whatever beer they've got on hand instead of the good stuff I could sell there."

Gwen laughed, too. "Let's cross that bridge when we get to it, shall we? And until then..." She stole another kiss. "Thank you. For dealing with my dad today, for this whole weekend. For everything."

"No, thank *you*. You turned my life upside-down and I had no idea how badly I needed that."

"We could do this for the rest of our lives, couldn't we? Just sit here going 'no, thank *you*?'"

"Not if you're going to go do the rock star thing, no. Or if I'm going to do the brewmaster thing, for that matter."

"Never mind," Gwen said. "The responsibility thing? That's gotten old now."

Bill laughed again, startled, and kissed her again. "No, it hasn't."

"No. And it's never going to." Gwen sighed happily, then got up and gestured to the band. "C'mon, everybody. Let's go talk to Mike Piccolo, and get the future started."

MADISON SQUARE GARDEN - 8 MONTHS
LATER

*P*enny hissed, "There are fifteen *thousand* people out there," and Gwen, standing with the rest of the band just before they went onstage, let out a hysterical giggle.

"Is it too late to back out now?"

"I would actually murder you," Myles said serenely, which made her giggle again. "Besides," he added, "technically they're not here for us."

"Oh thanks a *lot*, that really helps!" He was right: the Sixty Pix were the opening act for a much bigger band, but it was still fifteen *thousand* people, give or take. And some of them were absolutely here for the Pix. Bill was there, for example, and so was his cousin Ashley, "Just this once," she'd said. Ripley, who had never been out of Colorado before and was basically exploding with excitement every time they went around a corner in New York City, had joined them, too. If nobody else had shown up, that would be enough, Gwen thought. Although it was considerably better that other people *had* shown up, if she was being honest with herself.

The band was meant to be on in three minutes, and the crowd had already begun to sing the chorus to *Not Again*, just like they'd done the first night in Renaissance. It was tradition now: Gwen actually couldn't remember a gig they'd played in the past eight months that hadn't started with the audience wooing them onto stage with that song. "You ready?"

Sandy, smiling, lifted her mic to her mouth and joined in the chorus. She hardly had a syllable out before the crowd's singing turned into an excited roar of anticipation, although within seconds they were singing again, ushering Sandy in. They broke into cheers again when she walked out on stage, though enough of them kept singing that the music rose and rebounded through the stadium. Gwen carefully dashed tears from her eyes. She found herself welling up every time this happened, and honestly hoped she'd never stop. It was a beautiful, powerful moment every night, and she loved it immensely.

Watching her bandmates go onto stage, one by one, being greeted, cheered, welcomed, and adored as they took their places, was maybe Gwen's single favorite part of every show. She knew—they all knew—that the noise was loudest for her, but she was just about comfortable with that now. It had been an insane eight months, with more publicity than even she could have imagined. Way, way more than the band had understood, even after she'd warned them. They'd come through it, though, and now Penny was heading onto the stage to rapturous cheers as she took her place in the lineup. It was all just about perfect.

She checked the pocket of her leather coat before it was her turn to bring the mic up and start singing. The little box she'd put there was still there, safe behind the zippered closure. She'd still been checking it all afternoon. Penny had told her she was going to blow the whole thing if she didn't cut it out, in fact, and the rest of the band, who were all in on it, had nodded. She still had her elbow pressed against it when she joined the first verse, and walked out on stage.

There was nothing, *nothing* like the rush of being greeted by so many people with such passion and enthusiasm. Nothing, Gwen thought, except the exact opposite of it: the safety and calm she found with her true love, because she still couldn't call him her fated mate and take it seriously. She waved at the crowd, pointing to people, finding Bill *in* the crowd—right up front where he always was, with their manager, Mike Piccolo, grinning hugely at his side. Those little rituals always helped her get her bearings early in a performance, but Gwen was surprisingly nervous when that first song ended and she stepped forward, first to shout out a greeting to the audience, then to grin and wait out cheers of welcome. "Before we really get started tonight, I want to ask somebody up on stage for a minute here."

Several thousand people volunteered at the tops of

their voices, and Gwen burst out laughing. "Sorry, sorry, I want to ask someone *specific* up on stage here. Bill Torben, can you come up?"

A spotlight flashed down to him, and Bill's eyes went huge. He stood frozen for half a second, staring up at her incredulously, before a massive grin split his face and he took the route security cleared for him so he could come up on stage. *He* didn't have a mic, so when he got up there to her, still grinning, he said, "Are you gonna do what I think you're gonna do?" and nobody else heard him.

She would absolutely never ask him to marry her in front of fifteen thousand people without clearing it with him beforehand. Or, at least, making sure he wanted to marry her. They'd talked about it almost since the beginning, and Bill had always been calm and confident about it all. *Yeah,* he said, *yeah, I'd love to get married when your career gives us a minute. I trust the mate bond, Gwen. We're meant to be together.*

So it wasn't a question of whether he'd say yes. But Gwen hadn't actually warned him she was going to propose tonight, so her nervous little grin had to be answer enough for him right then. The whole crowd had gone absolutely silent in an anticipatory hush so tense Gwen could practically hear fifteen thousand contained squeals of excitement. Surprised to find her hands shaking, she managed to fumble the ring box out of her pocket, and as she knelt on the stage, absolute pandemonium broke loose in the stadium. "Yeah," she said underneath the impossible roar. "I'm gonna do what you think I'm gonna do. Will you marry me, William Robert Torben?"

Bill didn't actually take the ring, or even the ring box. He just scooped Gwen up entirely, effortlessly as always, and spun her around on the stage to the sound of thousands and thousands of cheers. "Yeah," he said in her ear. "Yes, Gwendolyn Louise Booker, I absolutely will. God, I love you. I love you so much."

"I love you too," she whispered joyfully. "Now put me down so I can put a ring on it, big man."

He put her down, and kissed her, then let her slide the diamond engagement ring onto his left hand, and gazed at it in wonder. It was a narrow band, particularly on his big hands, with three inset diamonds that would match the wedding ring it came with. "That's gorgeous," he said in awe, as if they were completely alone. "It's perfect."

Relief crashed through her and came out in a giggle. "Oh good. I spent ages looking for it. C'mon, let's show it to the people."

She caught his hand and turned toward the hysterical audience, holding up Bill's hand to show off the ring. The noise quadrupled, which should have been impossible, and they were both laughing when Bill lowered his hand, took a mic, and in a low, almost shy, voice, said, "Thank you. I'm gonna go blush in a corner now so you guys can get back to the main event."

Gwen blurted, "No wait!" and grabbed his hand again, smiling both at him at the crowd. "No, wait. We've got a new song for you tonight, and I want to sing it for you right now. It's called *Happily Ever After.*"

The words didn't matter, she realized later, and that was probably a good thing, because she could barely hear herself over the endlessly cheering crowd. What mattered was the moment, and the forever that came next, and Bill's blush, and the stars in his eyes as she sang to him.

It didn't hurt, of course, that the song charted at number six nation-wide the next week, and there was really nothing better than everyone joining in when she sang it again at their wedding six months later. Footage from the wedding became the song's official video, and that, Gwen thought, really was a perfect happily ever after.

~

ACKNOWLEDGMENTS

My profound thanks to early readers Kathy Rogers, Edward Ellis, Sarah Brooks, Mary Hargrove, Kate Sheehy, and Nicole, for catching numerous typos and other errors in this book! Any other unnoticed mistakes are obviously entirely my own fault.

Further thanks are due to Malice & Mayhem Book Covers for the absolutely delightful cover design for this book and series.

-Catie

ABOUT THE AUTHOR

Some say Murphy Lawless is the descendant of Irish gangsters, exiled to Australia, who has made good on the family name. It's probably true*.

But then, others claim that Murphy was a spy for the Allies during the war. Stories are told of daring rescues of intrepid reporters from almost certain death, but Murphy has never admitted to anything. Still others say Lawless studied with a local tribe for years after crash-landing in the untamed wilds, having accepted a dare from a pilot of ill repute, and came away from the experience a kinder, wiser, and gentler soul.

Even now, though, the most widely held belief is that Lawless left Australia as a mere slip of a thing, and made a fortune in the wilds of the Alaskan oil fields before realizing that romance was the ultimate adventure. Murphy now writes passionate, fun-filled stories of paranormal romance and destined love.

*Probably.

You can find Murphy at catiemurphy.com, Patreon, and at her newsletter, which is by far the best way to have up-to-date information delivered straight to you!